"I have a problem that is threatening to cause me a certain amount of—embarrassment," Andreas began.

"I do have a workable solution, however," he said, glancing back at his glass and tipping it slightly so the golden liquid clung to the sides. "But to have any chance of success it requires a wife and child. Meeting you today," he went on levelly, "seeing where you live and, more important, how you live—it suddenly occurred to me that you may well be the ideal candidate for the role...."

"What role?" she asked, utterly lost as to what he was getting at.

He grimaced into his glass, she presumed because she was forcing him into being more explicit about what he meant.

"As my wife," he enlightened her. Then, when she still continued to stand there blank-faced and frowning in bewilderment, he lifted his eyes until they were fixed sardonically on hers and said, "I am asking you to marry me, Claire...."

GREEK TYCOONS

**They're the men who have everything—
except a bride...**

Wealth, power, charm—what else could a
heart-stoppingly handsome tycoon need? Meet
Andreas, Nikolas, Constantine and Dio, four
gorgeous Greek billionaires who are in need
of wives.

Look out for their stories, written by your
favorite authors, in which each tycoon meets his
match and decides that he *has* to have her...
whatever it takes!

Look out next month for
The Millionaire's Virgin
by Anne Mather

Michelle Reid

THE TYCOON'S BRIDE

GREEK
TYCOONS

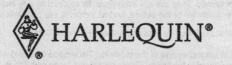

HARLEQUIN®

TORONTO • NEW YORK • LONDON
AMSTERDAM • PARIS • SYDNEY • HAMBURG
STOCKHOLM • ATHENS • TOKYO • MILAN • MADRID
PRAGUE • WARSAW • BUDAPEST • AUCKLAND

ISBN 0-373-12106-7

THE TYCOON'S BRIDE

First North American Publication 2000.

This edition published by arrangement with Harlequin Books S.A.

CHAPTER ONE

'ADOPTION?' Claire repeated in dismay. 'You want me to give Melanie away to strangers?'

Standing there, white-faced and shaking in the shabby sitting room of her equally shabby little flat, Claire stared at her aunt as if she had just turned into a real live she-devil. In truth, she was having trouble believing that any of this was really happening. In the last few tragic weeks it felt as if her whole life had been wrenched out from under her.

Now this, she thought wretchedly. 'I am going to pretend you never said that, Aunt Laura,' she said, cuddling the sleeping baby just that little bit closer as if trying to shield her from what was being proposed here.

'No, you're not,' her aunt countered sternly. 'You're going to listen to me. Do you honestly think I would be suggesting this if I believed you were coping?'

'I *am* coping!' Claire angrily insisted.

Wearing a pin-neat chic little two-piece grey suit and with her perfectly made up face and elegantly groomed blonde hair, Laura Cavell only needed to send her coldly fastidious eyes on a brief scan of their surroundings to completely denounce that declaration.

The place was in a mess, every available space cluttered with all the usual baby paraphernalia—the floor, the chairs, the unit tops in the attached tiny kitchen. It was only October but the notoriously unpredictable British weather was already wintry. Yet what small amount of heat there was coming from the electric fire was being blocked off behind a clotheshorse laden with wet baby clothes. The washing had to be dried somehow and Claire had no other way of doing it now she could no longer afford to use the laundrette in the high street. So the windows were steamed up, the air inside the chilly little room damp with hanging condensation.

Claire herself looked no better, her once outstandingly pretty face ravaged by too much grief, by too much worry, and by too many disturbed nights caused by a baby who only seemed to sleep when she was holding her.

'I only asked you for help with my rent, for goodness' sake,' she mumbled defensively, feeling like a stray cat that had dared to beg at a queen's front door.

'And sometimes people have to be cruel to be kind,' her aunt replied with a cold little shrug of her elegant shoulders. 'If that means I have to use ruthless methods to make you see the error in what you're trying to do here, then so be it.'

Which, Claire presumed, was her way of saying that she wasn't going to part with a single penny. But then, Aunt Laura had never been known for her charity.

'Melanie isn't even your child, Claire!'

'But she is my sister!' Claire angrily flashed back. 'How can you want to have her taken away from me?' It was a cry from the heart—a copiously bleeding heart that had known too much pain and grief over the last half year.

Her aunt winced—but her stance didn't alter. 'Your *half*-sister,' she corrected her. 'You don't even know who her father is,' she added, her red-painted mouth pursing with real distaste as she glanced down at the dark-haired, olive-skinned baby cradled in Claire's arms.

'What difference is that supposed to make?' Claire demanded, her blue eyes widening in affront at the rude remark. So, her mother had a fling with a Spanish waiter—so what? she wanted to shout. At least she'd still been able to attract a man—which was something after what she had been through with Claire's father! 'Melanie is still my flesh and blood, and I am still hers!' she declared, only just managing to bite back the angry reminder that her aunt was supposed to be their flesh and blood also!

Not that it had ever shown. Claire's mother had always

said that Aunt Laura had no heart to speak of. She was hard, she was tough, and the fact that she held down a very important job playing PA to the top dog at one of Europe's biggest merchant banks meant that she was also totally dedicated to her career.

The moment that Claire had dared to ask for help, she must have been racking her brains looking for a solution that would put an end to what she must be seeing as the beginning of years of hassle. So, to a woman who had found it very easy to sacrifice love, marriage and the prospect of her own children for the sake of that career, telling her own niece to give her sister away came easy to Aunt Laura.

Claire felt sick to her stomach.

'You're only twenty-one years old, damn it!' Aunt Laura sighed out impatiently when she caught a glimpse of Claire's expression. 'Until a month ago you were still a student. Now you've dropped out of university but you have no job,' she listed. 'No means whatsoever to support yourself, never mind a small baby! And now you tell me you can't even afford to pay the rent on this awful place!'

'I will find a job soon enough, I'm certain of it,' Claire stated proudly.

'A job doing what?' she was instantly challenged. 'Waiting at tables like that—child's father did? Cleaning floors? Skivvying for others when you could be doing what your mother wanted you to do, and getting your degree? And who is going to look after Melanie while you do scrub floors?' her aunt pushed on remorselessly. 'It takes a lot of money to employ a good baby-minder, Claire,' she warned. 'Your mother's estate barely left enough to bury her.'

The derision in that final remark cut Claire right to the quick. 'I have rights! I must have rights!' she cried. 'Surely the State will help me!'

'Of course,' her aunt agreed. 'But only as much as it absolutely has to do. The days are long gone when the State was prepared to pay up without much of a murmur. They encourage self-help these days—which is just another way of telling you to go away and get on with it,' she derided. 'And Melanie has rights too, you know; you seem to have overlooked that. Do you think *she* is going to thank you for bringing her up in poverty when she could be living with the kind of people who could give her everything?'

With the sheer brutality of her aunt's words scoring deep grooves into her already lacerated soul, Claire reeled away in an agony of mind-numbing confusion.

Would it be better for Melanie if she gave her up? she actually found herself wondering. Suddenly she was starting to see the future through the baby's eyes. And her aunt could well be telling the truth; Melanie would have no grounds to thank her for condemning her to the kind of life she could provide for her.

Silently she moved across the room to go and place the sleeping baby in her crib in the corner. She was so thin now that the pair of jeans and stretch-cotton blouse she was wearing were hanging on her body. Only a couple of months ago they would have been as tightly fitting as you would have expected any healthy young woman's clothes to be.

But a couple of months ago Melanie had not been born. And Claire's mother had still been here, happily looking forward to giving birth to a new life, which she'd seen as the path to a whole new beginning, after what the previous few years had put them through.

Just three years ago Claire had been the only child of two utterly doting parents. Then her father had died at his own hand when he couldn't face the fact that his business had failed, taking just about everything they owned along with it. They'd lost their home, their furniture—even most of their clothes had to be sold to pay back their debtors. By then they had moved from the Holland Park area of London into rented accommodation here in the East End.

Victoria Stenson had never really recovered from the way her husband of more than twenty years had bailed out of life, leaving her to pick up the pieces. On top of all that, she'd had to watch so-called friends melt clean away as her circumstances altered. Claire had had to leave her private school to finish her final year of education at the local state school. She too had had to watch her friends disappear in much the same way her mother had done.

It had been a tough, painful time that left Victoria Stenson feeling very disillusioned and bitter. She'd had to find a job, which, having spent the last twenty years of her life being taken care of, wasn't at all easy. Oddly enough, it was Aunt Laura who'd helped then. She'd found her sister a job working in an up-market fashion boutique where her natural flare for style and what suited people had come in useful.

But then, Victoria Stenson had been a very classy lady. As a tall and slender natural toffee-blonde, at forty-two years old she had still been a very attractive woman who proved to be very good at her new job. So when the lady who owned the boutique had suddenly taken ill and could not go on a planned trip to Madrid to check out one of her fashion suppliers, she'd felt no qualms in sending Victoria in her place.

The rest was history. By the time she'd come home again, Claire could not believe the change in her mother. She'd looked almost happy; more relaxed, more—at peace with herself. A couple of weeks later she'd found out why.

'I'm pregnant,' her mother had announced. And eight months later little Melanie was born. Small, sweet, olive-skinned and with a crop of black hair that they'd both found so comical when compared with their own fair colouring. It was love at first sight for all three of them.

They'd brought Melanie home here to this small flat with its two small bedrooms and tiny kitchen and bathroom. A couple of weeks later Victoria had gone back to work. It was August, and Claire was on her long summer break from university, so it had worked well that she could care for Melanie while her mother was out. They would have to find a baby-minder later—they had been aware of that—but for now they were both happy to share the caring between them and all in all things were beginning to look up for them, they'd thought.

Then tragedy had struck yet again. Victoria Stenson had suffered a massive haemorrhage that she'd never recovered from, leaving Claire shell-shocked and utterly grief-stricken, with a baby to care for and nothing much else to help her to do it.

Outside a car horn sounded. Behind Claire, her aunt Laura took a glance at her wristwatch and frowned. 'I've got to go,' she murmured impatiently. 'Oh—for goodness' sake,' she then snapped out. 'Will you leave the child alone for a moment and listen to me?'

As if she could actually feel her aunt's animosity towards her, the baby let out a soft yelp. It was purely instinctive for Claire to reach down and brush a soothing caress across the baby's petal-soft cheek, and as she did so a well of love came surging up inside her.

It wasn't fair, she thought tragically. It just wasn't fair what life was throwing at her! She wanted to keep Melanie with her! She wanted her mother back. She wanted her father back. She wanted her life back how it used to be before all of these horrible things began to happen.

'What are our options?' she questioned thickly, tears clearly not far away.

Behind her, her aunt sensed success coming closer and smothered a smile of satisfaction. 'There are waiting lists longer than you can imagine of childless couples who would be very grateful to you for—'

'I don't want gratitude,' Claire cut in, straightening to slice the older woman to ribbons with a razor of a look.

'No.' Wrong move, Aunt Laura realised. 'People who would give her a loving home, then,' she quickly backtracked. 'And a loving family life with all the security that comes along with that.'

But I would not have a place in her life, Claire thought bleakly. And tried to imagine strange arms cradling her sister, strange hands caring for her, feeding her, clothing her—loving her...

A cold sense of despair went chasing through her system, her eyes blurring as the tears tried to follow.

'There are discreet ways of going about it,' her aunt was saying. 'Private agencies that only accept the very best of society onto their books. The kind of people who would make sure Melanie wanted for nothing for the rest of her life. Surely it is at least worth considering the idea—if only for Melanie's sake...'

For Melanie's sake. Having found the right button to push, the super-sharp PA to one of Europe's top bankers was now using it ruthlessly.

'You could go back to university and finish your degree,' Aunt Laura continued. 'I would be prepared to help you to do that, because I think it's the right thing for you to do. But not this, Claire,' she murmured, with another contemptuous scan of their surroundings. 'I will not help you to wreck two lives when both you and Melanie deserve better than this...'

Melanie.

'I'll—think about it,' Claire heard herself whisper. But even as she said the dreadful words it felt as if someone was reaching down inside her and ripping her bleeding heart from her breast.

'Good,' her aunt murmured approvingly. 'While you do that, I will approach some of the agencies for you,' she offered. 'See what is required and how m—'

The car horn sounded again, cutting her off mid-word. And, on a small sigh of irritation, Laura Cavell glanced at her niece, saw the dreadful misery now apparent on her pale face—and relented a little. Opening her small clutch purse, she withdrew a slender leather wallet.

'Look, take this...' she said, sliding a folded wad of paper money out of the wallet which she placed on the arm of the sofa. 'It should see you through until I can get back to you in a couple of days. By then I will expect you to have made a decision.'

Staring at the money, Claire nodded. 'Thank you,' she breathed, but they both knew she didn't really feel grateful.

'Please try to think with your head, not your heart, Claire,' was her aunt's final volley as she walked to the door.

Then she was gone, leaving Claire standing there staring at the money she had left behind her.

Her thirty pieces of silver, she likened tragically, and had to wrap her slender arms around her body in an effort to still the icy chill that suddenly ran through her blood.

Because that's what this money is, she acknowledged as she made herself walk forward and sit down beside the wad of notes. The price of betrayal of those we love most.

With her heart throbbing dully in her breast, she reached out with a hand and picked up the folded wad with the grim intention of finding out how much that betrayal was worth these days.

But she didn't even get as far as counting the notes when something dropped out from in between them that had her launching herself off the sofa and running to yank open the door.

Her flat was on the first floor. She made a dive for the stairwell just as the main front door downstairs slammed shut. Muttering a couple of choice curses that would have drawn her mother's wrath if she had been alive to hear them, Claire began racing down the stairs in pursuit of Aunt Laura with the wad of bills still clutched in her hand—and with them a gold plastic credit card.

An ice-cold north-easterly wind hit her full in the face as she dragged open the heavy front door. She paused and shivered, her thin blouse no protection as she stood there at the top of the steps urgently searching the street in front of her for a glimpse of her aunt Laura's distinctive figure.

It was a narrow street but a busy one, used as a cut-through between two main highways. It was lined on both sides by high Victorian-style terraced houses that would once have been quite elegant until time and decay, and greedy property developers, had turned them into cheap tenement dwellings.

The two rows of cheap and old cars parked up against the kerb reflected the quality of the tenants. So the long, sleek limousine Claire could see her aunt climbing into stood out like a rich dark hybrid rose amongst a tangle of briar. It was parked on the other side of the street and facing towards her with its engine already running.

'Aunt Laura!' she called out, trying to catch her attention before she disappeared into its spacious rear compartment. But the wind whipped her voice away, the rear door closed her aunt inside and almost instantly the limousine inched into movement.

Without thinking what she was doing, Claire darted forwards, the thin-soled ballet slippers she wore around the flat no protection from the cold, hard pavement as she ran across it then out into the street with the intention of stopping the car before it had gained momentum.

What came next happened so very quickly that the whole became lost in a blur of confusing sounds and images. She had a feeling, for instance, that she would remember to her dying day the sound of a horn shrilling furiously at her. Just as she would always have a rather curious image of her own golden hair fanning out in a shimmering arc around her face and shoulders as her head spun to register the delivery van bearing inexorably down on her.

Then there was the ear-piercing sound of screeching brakes, the acrid smell of burning rubber, and the warning cries from helpless onlookers who were seeing as clearly as she was seeing what was about to happen.

And even as the adrenaline did the exact opposite of what she needed it to do for her and froze her utterly to the spot instead of jolting her into taking avoiding action—she still managed to note the terrible look on the delivery driver's face when he too realised that he was not going to be able to stop without hitting her.

Yet—interestingly—the impact itself she barely registered. She felt a thump to her right-hand side, but not the pain that should have come with it.

The next thing she knew, she was lying in the road and a dark-eyed stranger was leaning over her while someone in the background was talking wildly in a choked, shocked, shaking voice. 'She just ran out in front of me!' he was saying over and over. 'I didn't stand a chance! She just ran out in front of me—she just ran out in front of me...'

Was he referring to her? Claire wondered dizzily, and on a frown of confusion attempted to sit up.

'Don't move,' a quiet voice commanded. Vaguely she registered the hint of a foreign accent, liked the deep velvet sound of it and smiled accordingly.

'OK,' she complied. Crazily, it really did seem that simple. She still felt nothing, and, in those first few conscious moments, she remembered nothing, which didn't seem to matter either. A strange state of mind, she decided—all fluffy and floaty.

'Am I dying or something?' she wondered curiously.

'Not while I am here to stop you,' replied the stranger.

She found herself smiling at that too. Arrogant devil, she thought. And became aware of a hand resting on one of her shoulders while another hand was dispassionately travelling all over her body as if it had every right to do something like that. Yet—oddly—she let him. Her worry-bruised deep blue eyes solemnly studied him as he carried out his examination. He wasn't young, she noted, but he wasn't exactly old either. And his skin—like his voice—was definitely foreign, bronzed and sleek, and he had a nicely defined mouth that, for some reason, she wanted to reach up and trace with her fingertips.

But really it was his eyes that held her attention. They were dark—so dark it was like looking into nothing.

Catching her studying him, he sent her a brief grim smile that made something alien stir inside her. She didn't understand it—didn't recognise the feeling, but it was disturbing enough to make her close her eyes and shut him out again as a wave of dizziness rolled over her.

She began to shiver suddenly—though she wasn't sure why unless the cold was beginning to get her—yet she didn't feel cold—not at all, actually—which was strange in itself considering the icy weather.

Something warm and silky landed on top of her, and she realised that he had taken off his jacket and covered her with it.

It was only then that it occurred to her that she shouldn't be lying here; that she had been in a hurry to get somewhere—though for the life of her she couldn't remember where she was supposed to be going.

'I said—don't move!' the deep voice insisted.

'Did I?' she asked, frowning confusedly because she certainly wasn't aware of moving.

In fact she didn't feel able to do anything very much— even breathing in air was strangely difficult. Her chest felt tight, her limbs heavy.

And for all she knew she could be very seriously injured. It was well documented, wasn't it—that the worse you were, the less you felt? 'My chest hurts,' she confided, meaning to reassure herself with that bit of information.

He didn't seem to understand that, though, because she heard his harsh expletive muttered beneath his breath. 'Has someone called the emergency services?' he demanded of— whoever. Claire wasn't sure who, nor cared that much really. But she did become aware of hurried footsteps coming towards her.

'I've seen to it,' another voice announced breathlessly. Then, 'I can't believe she just ran out in the street like that!' the voice added angrily.

Her aunt. Claire winced on a rush of total recall.

'Did that hurt?' the stranger enquired concernedly. He was touching her right wrist, and, yes, it did hurt, she realised belatedly. But that wasn't why she had winced.

A pair of handmade Italian court shoes appeared beside her. 'What made you do such a stupid thing?' her aunt demanded furiously.

Lifting up her injured wrist, she opened her fingers with effort. Lying there, half hidden amongst the crumpled wad of notes, was her aunt's plastic gold card. 'You left this behind,' she explained. 'I thought you might be needing it...'

For the space of thirty long, taut seconds, no one else made a single solitary sound as they stared at the gold card in Claire's palm.

Then the stranger spoke. 'You know this girl?' he demanded sharply of her aunt Laura. 'She is the niece you came here to see this morning?'

'Yes,' Laura Cavell confirmed with enough reluctance to make Claire wince all over again.

How can anyone be so uncomfortable with the fact that they possess family? Claire wondered bleakly. And at last managed to pull herself into a sitting position while everyone's attention was elsewhere.

'Look, Mr Markopoulou...' Aunt Laura was saying, sounding unusually anxious for her. 'If you want to leave this situation to me now, you could still just manage to catch your flight to Madrid.'

That was the moment when Claire realised that the tall, dark stranger was none other than Aunt Laura's hot-shot tycoon employer! No wonder she is sounding so anxious, she mused ruefully.

'I thought I told you not to move,' the dark voice censured.

'I'm fine now—really,' she lied. 'No one needs to miss their flight. In fact, I think I would like to get up now.'

'I think not,' the stranger drawled, his black eyes autocratic. 'You will remain exactly where you are until the emergency services arrive to check you over.'

No way, Claire thought. If they took her to hospital then Aunt Laura would have her certified as unfit to take care of Melanie before she could even turn around!

Then, 'Oh, no!' she gasped, scrambling shakily to her feet. She'd left the baby in the flat on her own!

Her head felt groggy, her shoulders stiff, and her insides were shaking so badly that they were making her feel sick.

'Where do you think you are going?' the stranger demanded, vaulting to his feet like a well-honed athlete.

'I have to go now,' she murmured hazily.

Barely registering the small crowd clustered around them, she took a few staggering steps forward—then remembered the gold card still clutched in her hand—the cause of all of this trouble in the first place, she acknowledged mockingly as she spun back towards Aunt Laura.

'Here...' she said, plucking the card out from amongst the crumpled bank notes and handing it over.

Her aunt took it in grim silence, her red-painted mouth tight with angry embarrassment.

Turning back to find the stranger had moved to stand directly in her path, Claire mumbled an awkward, 'Thanks for your trouble,' went to divert around him only to come to yet another confused halt when she noticed the pristine whiteness of his shirt.

No jacket...

Glancing behind her, she was appalled to see his jacket lying on the road where it had slid away from her unnoticed when she'd got up. 'Oh—I'm so sorry!' she gasped, making a move to go and collect it.

He got there before her, though. Tall, dark, whipcord lean, he bent to retrieve it in one smooth movement.

'I'm so very sorry.' Claire apologised a second time.

His idle shrug dismissed the oversight. 'Here...' Instead the jacket landed back around her shoulders. 'You seem to need it more than I do at this moment,' he explained. Then he bent his head towards her to add gently, 'You are shivering.'

'But...' The rest of what she had been going to say got lost in a sudden wave of dizziness. Her wrist was hurting, her chest felt very tight, and her head was beginning to thump. She became aware of a cluster of blurred faces all staring at them in rapt curiosity.

An arm came gently about her shoulders. 'Come on,' her aunt Laura's boss said coolly. 'Show me where you live and I will see that you get there...'

'It really isn't necessary,' she protested.

'It is, I assure you,' he insisted rather grimly. 'For I am not leaving until I am sure you have been checked out professionally.'

And it was amazing—but he meant it! He even sounded as though he cared! Hot tears suddenly filled her eyes, though she had no idea why they did. 'It isn't even as though it was your car that hit me!' she choked out in something between a sob and a protest.

'No, my van did that,' another male voice intruded. 'Are you sure you're all right?' the newcomer then enquired worriedly.

'Yes—really.' Seeing the shock still whitening the driver's face, she sent him a reassuring smile. 'A bit winded,' she confessed. 'But otherwise I'm OK. I'm sorry I was so stupid.'

'No problem—no problem,' the other man said, and he walked off looking relieved to be getting away from it all without getting into more trouble.

Claire felt another wave of dizziness wash over her. The arm resting across her shoulders suddenly became supportive. 'Lead the way, Miss Cavell,' his grim voice commanded.

Silent as a grave and stiff-backed as a corpse, Laura Cavell stalked into the house while they followed behind her. Her aunt was going to despise her for showing her up like this in front of her boss, Claire thought wearily as they trod the stairs. 'You don't have to go to this much trouble, you know,' she muttered uncomfortably. 'I really am all right.'

'No, you are not,' the man beside her replied. 'Your right wrist is injured. You have a cut on your head that needs attention. And when you breathe you gasp—which suggests you may have cracked a rib or two.'

An injured wrist. A cracked rib or two. Claire closed her eyes and wondered bleakly when something good was going to happen.

There didn't seem to be much use in hoping for it, she decided heavily. Things around her seemed to be going from bad to worse with every passing minute.

When they reached her flat she broke free from him so she could precede him through the door. Laura was standing by the clothes-horse—valiantly trying to hide it, Claire suspected, with the first hint of humour she'd felt in weeks.

Then, from behind her, she could sense her aunt's boss running his gaze over his shabby surroundings and all hint of humour completely left her. Outside in the street stood a limousine belonging to a man who was rich enough to travel everywhere in absolute luxury. His clothes shrieked of bespoke tailoring. No doubt his many homes were large and palatial, and here he was, Claire concluded, standing in what was probably the shabbiest abode it had ever been his misfortune to experience.

Shame washed through her. Why she didn't know, because the feelings of a complete stranger really shouldn't matter to her. But something made her turn around to confirm the look of distaste she just knew would be written all over his lean, dark, super-elegant features.

It was there.

She felt hurt, so very hurt.

Then, as if to completely demolish her, a soft snuffling sound came from the corner of the room, and the way his expression altered to a look of shocked horror as he accurately registered just what that sound belonged to finally wrecked what was left of her fragile composure. In an act of teeth-gritting defiance, she whipped off his jacket and threw it at him.

Startled, his black eyes widened on her. 'You don't have to come in,' she clipped, suddenly alight with a bristling hostility. 'And actually I would prefer it if you didn't.'

'Claire!' her aunt objected furiously.

'I don't care!' she flashed. 'I just want you both to get out of here!'

Angrily she spun away to hurry over to the small baby crib where Melanie was still sleeping peacefully, she was relieved to discover.

But the tears weren't far away. She could feel them coming as she stood there leaning over the crib with an aching wrist hanging limply by her side and her ribcage beginning to pain her badly.

Behind her the silence went on and on. They hadn't gone and she wished that they would because she was beginning to feel rather hot and shaky.

'Please go,' she pleaded. Then, without warning, she fainted.

Maybe he saw it coming. Maybe he was already walking over to where she stood without her being aware that he'd moved. Whatever, as Claire felt herself going, as the blood slowly drained away from her head and her legs began to go limp, a pair of arms came securely around her, and the last thing she recalled was hearing the distinctive wail of an ambulance siren as she slumped heavily against him.

After that everything became a bit hazy, and she didn't really start making sense of what was happening to her until she was travelling in the ambulance—accompanied by none other than Aunt Laura's boss who was cradling Melanie.

But no Aunt Laura.

'She will be joining us later,' the stranger replied when Claire queried her aunt's absence. 'She needed to attend to some urgent business.'

Frowning at him through huge, pain-bruised blue eyes, she wondered why he wasn't taking care of his own urgent business. But their arrival at the local hospital forestalled any more conversation between them when she was taken away to be examined and x-rayed.

Her ribs, she discovered, were only bruised, but her wrist was a different matter. A broken scaphoid, the doctor called it, and they would have to put her out briefly to reset it.

'What about Melanie?' she fretted as the pre-med they had given her began to send her brain fuzzy. 'How am I going to cope with my wrist in plaster? Where's Aunt Laura?'

'If you want your aunt here, then I will get her here,' a deep voice that was starting to sound very familiar quietly promised. She had expected Aunt Laura's boss to melt away once they reached the hospital, but to her surprise he had stayed with her the whole time.

'No,' she sighed in shaky refusal, shifting restlessly where she lay because he didn't understand. It wasn't that she wanted her aunt—she just needed to know where she was and what she was doing because she didn't trust her not to take matters into her own hands where Melanie was concerned, while she was in no fit state to stop her.

'Don't let her take her away from me,' she mumbled slurredly.

'I won't,' the voice promised.

That was the last thing she remembered for the next hour or so, so she had no idea that he continued to stand there beside her bed grimly watching over her until they came to wheel her away.

When she did eventually resurface, it was to find herself lying in a small side room with her wrist encased in its new plaster cast and secured by a sling. They had left her fingers and thumb free at least, she noticed—not that she felt overwhelmed with gratitude for that because she knew she still wasn't going to be able to handle a baby.

What did concern her was that it was going to take up to eight weeks to mend.

Eight weeks…

Sighing heavily, she closed her weary eyes and tried pretending that this was all just a bad dream.

'Worrying already?' a deep voice dryly intruded.

CHAPTER TWO

CLAIRE'S eyes flicked open, something disturbingly close to pleasure feathering across her skin as a tall, dark figure loomed up in front of her in the very disturbing form of Aunt Laura's hot-shot tycoon banker.

'How are you feeling?' he enquired politely.

'Dopey,' she replied, with a shy little grimace.

His dark head nodded in understanding. 'Give yourself time to recover a little from the anaesthetic,' he advised. 'Then—if you feel up to it—they say you can go home.'

Home... That sounded good. So good in fact that she made herself sit up and slide her feet to the ground. It was only then that she realised what a poor state her clothes were in. Her jeans were scored with dust and tar from the road, and her blouse had managed to lose half of its buttons.

No wonder he threw his jacket over me, she thought wryly, making a half-hearted attempt to tidy herself. But it was difficult to look pin-neat after the kind of day that she'd had, she decided heavily. While this man, whose eyes she could sense were watching her so intently, still looked elegant and sleek and clean even though he had spent most of the day rescuing fallen maidens, abandoned babies, and—

'Where's Melanie?' she asked sharply, unable to believe she had been so irresponsible as to not give the poor baby a single thought until now!

For the first time today, he suddenly looked cross. 'I would have expected by now that you would trust me to ensure your child is perfectly safe and well taken care of,' he clipped out impatiently.

'Why?' Claire immediately challenged that. 'Because my aunt Laura works for you?'

23

Something made his broad shoulders flex in sudden tension, though what made them do it Claire had no idea, but she felt her own tension rise in response to it.

'Just because you were gracious enough to pick me up and dust me off, then condescended to accompany me here instead of going off to Milan, that does not automatically win trust, you know,' she pointed out, coming upright on decidedly shaky legs.

'Madrid,' he corrected her absently—as if it really mattered!

'I don't know you from Adam,' Claire continued as if he hadn't spoken. 'For all I know you may be one of those weirdos that prey on innocent young females in vulnerable situations!'

A wild thing to say—a terrible thing to say considering what he *had* done for her today. Watching the way his elegant frame stiffened in affront, Claire was instantly contrite.

But as she opened her mouth to apologise he beat her to it—by retaliating in kind.

'Young you may be,' he grimly conceded. 'What are you, after all—not much more than eighteen? And vulnerable you certainly are at the moment—one only has to look at your face to know that a relatively minor road accident was not enough to cause quite that amount of fatigue in one so young. But innocent?' he questioned with cutting cynicism. 'One cannot be innocent *and* give birth to a child, Miss Stenson. It is, believe me, a physical impossibility.'

Two things hit her simultaneously as she stood there absorbing all of that. One was the obvious fact that he had got her age wrong. And the other was his mistaken belief that Melanie was her daughter!

Had Aunt Laura not bothered to explain anything to him? she wondered. And who the hell did he think he was, standing in judgement over her, anyway?

'I am not eighteen—I am twenty-one!' she corrected him angrily. 'And Melanie is not my daughter—she's my sister!

Our mother died, you see, just two weeks after giving birth. And if you hadn't been so quick to send my aunt off to do whatever business you felt was more important to her than we are,' she railed on, regardless of the clear fact that she had already managed to turn him to stone, 'then maybe she would have had the chance to explain all of this to you, so you didn't have to stand here insulting me! And my innocence or lack of it is none of your damned business,' she tagged on for good measure.

At that point, and giving neither of them a chance to recover, the door swung open and a nurse walked in carrying Melanie.

'Ah, you're awake.' She smiled at Claire, seemingly unaware of the sizzling atmosphere she had walked into. Stepping over to the bed, she gently laid the sleeping baby down on it. 'She has been fed, changed and generally spoiled,' she informed them as she straightened. 'So you need not concern yourself about her welfare for the next few hours.'

'Thank you,' Claire murmured politely. 'You've all been very kind.'

'No problem,' the nurse dismissed. 'If you feel up to it, you can leave whenever you want,' she concluded, and with a brisk squeak of rubber on linoleum was gone again—leaving a tension behind her that stuck like glue to Claire's teeth and her throat, making it impossible for her to speak or swallow.

So instead she moved to check on the baby. As the nurse had assured her, Melanie looked perfectly contented. Her left hand went out to gently touch a petal-soft cheek while he looked on in grim silence.

'I apologise,' he murmured suddenly. 'For the—altercation earlier. I had no right to remark upon either your life or your morals. And I certainly had no right to make certain assumptions about either you or your situation. I am, in fact, ashamed of myself for doing so.'

Quite a climb-down, Claire made note, nodding in acceptance of his apology. 'Who are you?' she then asked curiously. 'I mean—what is your name? It seems crazy that we have spent almost half the day together and I don't even know your name.'

'Your aunt never mentioned me?' he questioned.

Claire shook her head. 'Only that she worked with the head of a merchant bank,' she told him.

He seemed to need a few moments to take this information in, which Claire thought was rather odd of him. 'My name is Andreas Markopoulou,' he then supplied. 'I am Greek,' he added, as though he felt it needed saying.

Feeling suddenly quite painfully at a loss as to what she was supposed to do with his name now that she had it, all Claire could come up with was another small nod of acknowledgement.

Consequently, the silence came back, but it was a different kind of silence now as they stood there eyeing each other as if neither quite knew what to do next. It was all very strange, very—hypnotic, Claire thought hazily.

Then he seemed to give himself a mental shake and stepped up to the other side of the bed. 'Maybe we should leave now,' he huskily suggested.

'Oh, yes,' she said, and bent with the intention of scooping Melanie up with her good arm.

But he stopped her. 'I will carry her,' he insisted, adding almost diffidently now that they seemed to be trying very hard not to tread on each other's feelings, 'Perhaps you would accept the use of my jacket again? The day is drawing in and it must be quite cold outside...'

A hesitant nod of agreement had him rounding the bed as he removed his jacket so he could place it across her slender shoulders, then he was turning to get Melanie. And without another word passing between them they made their way to the hospital exit.

Just as he had predicted, it was cold outside, but within

seconds of them appearing his car came sweeping into the kerb just in front of them. As soon as the car stopped, the driver's door shot open and a steely-haired short, stocky man in a grey chauffeur's uniform stepped out.

Rounding the car's shiny dark red bonnet, he touched his peaked hat in greeting and deftly opened the rear door, politely inviting Claire to get into the car.

Wincing a little because her bruised ribs didn't like the pressure placed on them to make the manoeuvre, it was a minute or two before she felt able to take in the sheer luxury of her surroundings—the soft kid leather upholstery and impressive amount of in-car communications hardware.

It all felt very plush, very decadent. Very—Andreas Markopoulou, Claire mused wryly as the door on the other side of the car opened and the man himself coiled his impressive lean length into the seat next to her—without Melanie.

'Be at ease,' he said before Claire could even voice the alarmed question forming on her lips. 'She is perfectly safe. See, I will show you...'

Reaching out towards his door panel, he pressed a button that sent the dark glass partition between them and the driver sliding smoothly downwards. Having to move carefully so it didn't hurt too much, Claire sat forward a little so she could peer over the front passenger seat—where she found Melanie snugly strapped into a baby car seat fixed to the seat next to the beaming driver.

A car seat just for Melanie? 'You really shouldn't have gone to so much trouble for us,' Claire mumbled awkwardly. 'You've done more than enough as it is.'

'It is nothing,' he dismissed, sitting back and pressing the button that brought the partition window sliding up again.

Claire was edging herself carefully back into her seat when a sudden thought hit her. 'That seat isn't new, is it?' she asked. 'You have borrowed it from someone?' Oh—please let him say it's borrowed! she prayed fervently.

But the arrogant look he levelled at her spoke absolute volumes, and had Claire stiffening in dismay. 'But the expense!' she cried. 'I won't be able to pay you back!'

'I was not expecting you to,' drawled a man to whom money had obviously never been a luxury he couldn't afford to toss away! And with a shrug that dismissed the whole subject as boring he turned his head to glance outside as the car slid into smooth motion.

But Claire couldn't let him just dismiss it like that. It wasn't right that he should fork out for anything for them! 'I will have to ask my aunt if she will reimburse you,' she decided stubbornly.

'Forget it,' he said.

'But I don't want to forget it!' she cried. 'I hate being beholden to anybody!'

Arrogantly, he ignored all of that. 'Please fasten your seat belt,' he instructed instead. Then, 'Leave it,' he advised when she opened her mouth to continue the argument, the sheer softness of his tone enough to still her tongue. 'It is done. The seat is bought. Further argument is futile...'

Lowering her face, Claire began attempting to fasten her seat belt around her with fingers that were suddenly shaking badly. In all her life she had never been spoken to quite like that, even by Aunt Laura, who could be intimidating enough.

'I can't do this!' she sighed after a few taut moments of hopeless fumbling that made her frustratingly aware of how incapacitated she was going to be with one hand rendered completely useless, and felt the tears that were too ready to appear just lately begin to fill her eyes again.

With a smooth grace, he leaned across the space separating them, took the belt from her trembling fingers and, carefully making sure that the belt sat low down on her body so that it missed both her ribs and her plaster-cast, he locked it into place.

He glanced up, saw the tears, and released a soft sigh. 'Don't get upset, because I have a tendency to cut into people,' he murmured apologetically. 'It is a—design fault in my make-up,' he explained sardonically. 'I dislike having my actions questioned, so I react badly. My fault—not yours...'

'You should not have spent money on us without my say-so,' Claire couldn't resist saying despite the fact that she seemed to know instinctively that—half apology or not—he wasn't going to like her resurrecting the argument.

Still, if he was angry, he managed to keep his voice level. 'Well, it is done now.' And although the remark was dismissive again at least he cloaked it in a gentler tone. 'How is your wrist?' he enquired, wisely changing the subject.

Glancing down to where the sling held the heavy plaster-cast against her slender body, she noticed an ugly swelling around the base of her thumb. 'It's OK,' she lied.

In fact it was throbbing quite badly now. But then, so was her head—and her ribcage. Closing her eyes, she let herself relax back into the seat, feeling so tired, so utterly used up now that she had an idea that if she was left to do it she could easily sleep for a whole year.

But she wasn't going to be able to sleep, was she? Instead she was going to have to come up with a way to take care of Melanie while her wrist was like this.

Out from behind the dull throb of her physical pain and her mental exhaustion her aunt Laura's rotten suggestion reared its ugly head. It was enough to make her open her eyes, make her sit up straight as aching muscles knotted up with stress. Unaware of the pair of black eyes that were observing her narrowly, her anxious gaze went dancing around as if on a restless search for deliverance.

'What's wrong?' he enquired levelly.

'Nothing.' She shook her head. For how could she tell him that his highly respected PA could be crass enough to want to give away one of her own nieces rather than help share responsibility for her? It was wicked, simply wicked.

Yet you said you were prepared to consider the option, Claire grimly reminded herself.

Her eyes grew stark, the tired bruising around the sockets becoming more pronounced as the weight of all her many problems began pressing on her once again.

Then other things began intruding on her consciousness. The fact, for instance, that the car was driving them through a part of London that was very familiar to her since she'd used to live around here until three years ago.

But that was a long way away from the East End district where she lived now. Frowning in puzzlement, she glanced around to find Andreas Markopoulou's fathomless black eyes fixed on her watchfully.

'This isn't the way to my flat.' She stated the obvious.

Those dark eyes didn't so much as flicker. 'No,' he confirmed, adding smoothly, 'This is the way to *my* home.'

His home... Claire repeated to herself, and tried to work out why he had used the words with the kind of emphasis that had set instincts firing out all kinds of warnings at her.

'Your driver is going to drop you off first,' she nodded, deciding that was what he had been implying.

But beside her the dark head shook. 'We are all going there,' he said, waited a few moments for his words to sink in—then added gently, 'I am taking you both home with me.'

'But—what for?' she demanded frowningly. 'Will my aunt Laura be there?'

There was a long pause when his eyes continued to hold hers but he didn't answer. He has a beautiful face, she found herself thinking. Good bones and skin and nicely balanced features. It was a shame the whole was spoiled by the cold mask he wore over it...

Then she blinked, realising that he still hadn't answered her but was just sitting there, watching her studying him, and by the sardonic gleam she could see lurking in his eyes he knew exactly what she was thinking but didn't give a damn.

Not just cold, she thought suddenly, but proud of it. And she shuddered as if something unholy had just reached out to brush its icy fingertips along her body.

The car came to a stop. 'We have arrived,' he announced, and leaned over to flick free her safety belt.

Instantly her skin began to prickle, her heartbeat picking up pace as a burst of alarm forced her into taking avoiding action by pressing her body back into the seat.

'Be calm,' he murmured dryly as he carefully guided the belt back into its housing so it didn't whip across her body. 'You truly have nothing to fear from me.'

No? Claire wished she could believe that—an hour ago she *would* have believed that! But since then something about this man had altered subtly and what really frightened her was that she just didn't understand what that something was!

Nikos, the chauffeur, was opening her door then, and offering to help her to alight. Feeling stubborn in the face of her own confusion, she ignored his outstretched hand and climbed out of the car under her own steam. But the effort took its toll, and she had to steady herself with her good hand on the bonnet of the car while her many aches and pains made their presence felt.

She knew this street, she realised, suddenly becoming aware of her surroundings. It was several streets up from the one where she used to live when her father was alive, though this part of Holland Park was a hundred times more exclusive.

But at least she knew where to run to if she needed to get away from here, she told herself. And with that consoling thought, she turned to watch the chauffeur release Melanie from her safety seat, while Andreas Markopoulou stood to one side of him, waiting to receive the baby into his arms.

The baby arrived, all cute and cosy wrapped in a shawl her mother had so painstakingly crocheted throughout her confinement. And, for some crazy, unexplainable reason, remembering that brought on a violent surge of possessive jealousy that made her want to reach out and snatch the baby from him!

Maybe he sensed her resentment, because he turned then, to glance at her sharply. 'OK?' he asked.

No, Claire thought. I am not OK. I want you to give me my baby sister then I want to go home, because every single instinct I possess is telling me I should not be going anywhere with you!

Aunt Laura—Aunt Laura… Like a chant devised to soothe the troubled spirit, she found herself using Aunt Laura's connection to them both as an excuse as to why she was allowing herself to be taken over like this.

'Let's go…' Her new guardian led the way towards one of the elegant town houses that stood in the middle of an elegant white-painted row.

The door fell open even as they arrived at it, a short plump lady with hair a similar colour to the chauffeur's appearing in the opening with a warmly expectant smile on her face. The moment she saw Melanie she let out a soft cry of delight, clapped her hands together then opened them up in greedy readiness to receive the baby.

'This is my housekeeper, Lefka,' Andreas Markopoulou informed Claire as he dutifully placed the baby in the other woman's arms. 'As you can see from her expression, she is ecstatic to be given this opportunity to take care of the child while you are here.'

'Oh, but—' Claire began to protest, but even as the words began to form on her lips the housekeeper began speaking over the top of her, in what Claire had to assume was Greek. Then, without a by-your-leave to anyone, she turned and proceeded to disappear with Melanie into the bowels of the house!

'Usually her manners are much better than that,' Andreas Markopoulou dryly remarked as they watched the woman go. 'No doubt she will recover them once her bout of ecstasy has subsided.' Then, more formally, he invited Claire to enter his home.

The interior was more or less what she had expected—

large and warm and beautifully furnished in a tasteful mix of modern and antique.

Light hands smoothly removed the jacket. Glancing up and around, she mumbled a wary, 'Thanks,' but felt uncomfortably lost without the jacket to hide in.

Leading the way across the square hallway, he opened a door and invited her to precede him through it. In silence she went, still telling herself that she was going to find her aunt Laura waiting there—*needing* to find her aunt Laura waiting there.

But, except for the obvious fact that this was a man's very comfortable study—with its roaring log fire, light-oak-panelled walls and heavy oak furniture—the room revealed no sign of Aunt Laura.

Behind her, the door closed. She turned to confront him.

'Where's my aunt?' she demanded.

Sleek black eyebrows shot up. 'I do not recall saying that your aunt would be here,' he replied, moving gracefully across the room to where a big solid desk stood with its top clear of papers.

Had he said it? Claire's brow puckered up as she tried to remember just what he had said about her aunt, and found she couldn't say for sure.

But the impression had been drawn, she was sure of it. 'Then why have you brought us here?' she asked, puzzled. 'If it wasn't to meet up with Aunt Laura?'

He had switched on a small laptop computer and was studying whatever had appeared on the screen while casually tapping at one of the keys—though his head lifted at the question, his dark eyes drifting up the full length of her then back down again in a way that raised every fine hair on her body. 'I would have thought that was obvious,' he replied, his attention already back on the computer screen again. 'You are a mess, quite frankly,' he stated bluntly. 'And in no fit state to take care of yourself, never mind a helpless young baby. So, for the time being at least, you will stay here with me.'

'But I don't want to stay here!' Claire cried, too horrified by the prospect to dress up her protest.

That brief grim smile of his that he liked to use so much registered her horror. 'I wasn't aware,' he drawled, 'that I was giving you a choice.'

No choice? Who did he think he was, for goodness' sake? 'It isn't your problem.' She flatly refused the offer. 'We will manage somehow,' she insisted with more confidence than she really felt. 'My aunt—'

'Your aunt,' he interrupted, 'is already out of the country. And since we both know that she would rather—break *both* wrists,' he said, with a telling glance at Claire's plaster-cast, 'than be forced to play housemaid to anyone, then I think we can take her out of the equation, don't you?'

Out of the country—out of the equation? 'But it's you who says where Aunt Laura goes!' she pointed out confusedly.

He didn't even deign to answer that. Instead he lost interest in whatever was written on the computer screen and snapped it shut then straightened to give Claire his full attention.

She was still standing where he had left her, looking pale, drawn, and totally bewildered. A short sigh whispered from him. 'Look—why don't you sit down?' he suggested. 'And at least allow me to call the kitchen and order you something to eat and drink. I have been with you for most of the afternoon but as far as I have seen you have only taken a couple of sips of water in all that time...'

As it was, she had already determined that she wasn't accepting anything else from this man until she knew just what it was that was going on here, so the desire to tell him where to put his offer was strong.

But she was thirsty and cold, and at this moment she was ready to kill for something hot inside her stomach. 'A cup of tea would be nice,' she nodded. 'Please,' she added belatedly.

Then—seemingly because she had given in to one craving—she found herself giving in to another. While he began talking into the telephone, she turned to walk over to where two dark red velvet recliners sat flanking the blazing log fire.

Sitting down hurt. But then, just about every muscle she possessed was beginning to ache now, and the other thing she really wished for was a long soak in a piping-hot bath.

No chance of that, though, she thought, glancing dully at her plastered wrist. 'Don't get it wet,' they'd said. 'Tape a plastic bag around it when you bathe.'

But who taped the plastic bag? she asked herself dully, closing her weary eyes as her body sank into the softest velvet. And how did she undress herself, wash and dry herself? How did she manage all of those other little necessities that she'd taken so much for granted until today?

'Claire...' a deep voice prompted softly.

Her eyes flicked open. Had she been asleep again? She wasn't sure. All she did know was that she felt warm and comfortable at last. As she turned her head against the back of the chair, her sleepy eyes met with fathomless dark ones.

'I'm sorry to disturb you,' he said. 'But Lefka needs to know how Melanie likes her formula milk prepared?'

Melanie's formula milk? she repeated sluggishly to herself. Oh, good grief! How could she—how could she have forgotten all about the poor baby—again?

Without thinking what she was doing, she jolted to her feet. 'Aggh!' she cried out, as pain went screaming round her system.

She had jarred her bruised ribs and she could hardly bear it!

Then he was right there beside her. His long-fingered hands slid around her narrow waist to offer support while her slender body shook with violent spasms as she stood there, half bent over, trying desperately to ride the storm.

'You little fool!' he muttered angrily.

'Sh-shut up,' she gasped, needing his reproof like a hole in the head right then.

Grimly, he was silenced. And for the next few minutes the only sound in the room was her fight with her own body. When it was eventually over, she wilted like a dying flower against his chest—then stayed there, feeling so utterly used up that it was a long while before she began to notice little things about him. Like the padded firmness of his breastplate acting as a cushion for her cheek. And the lean tightness of his waist where her good hand had decided to come to rest. He felt big and warm and very tough, and there was a faint spicy smell floating all around her. It was pleasantly intoxicating.

'There is nothing of you,' he grunted.

And broke the spell.

'I'm all right now,' she said, pulling carefully away from him.

He let her go, his hands dropping slowly to his sides while he continued to stand there at the ready—in case she did anything else just as stupid.

'Melanie's formula,' she prompted flatly. 'I didn't bring any out with me.' No formula, no bottles, no nappies, nothing. 'I'll have to go home.'

'We have everything you will need right here,' he assured her.

Now what was that supposed to mean? she wondered wearily, sensing another battle in the offing. 'Don't tell me you've been out and bought the whole lot along with the car seat!' she sighed out heavily.

He didn't even deign to answer that. 'I will take you to the kitchen so you can show Lefka what she has to do.'

It was like dealing with an armoured tank driver, she thought grimly. What he didn't want to bother with, he rolled right over!

'Lead the way,' she said heavily, letting him have that small victory—for Melanie's sake, she told herself as she followed him out of the study and down the hallway towards the rear of the house.

The kitchen was a housewife's dream, all lovingly waxed wood and red quarry-tiled flooring. There was a huge Aga sitting in what Claire presumed had once been the fireplace, the kind of smells coming from the pots busy simmering away on its top enticing enough to make her stomach cry out in appeal.

A young dark-haired woman of around her own age was standing near to the Aga, close to a baby's travel cot. As Claire made eagerly for the cot, the young woman melted silently away.

Melanie was lying there, wide awake for once, and looking curiously around her. She had been changed, she noticed, and was wearing what looked like a brand-new sleep suit in the softest shade of pink that showed off her olive skin and jet-black cap of fine straight hair.

There was nothing about her that resembled her dead mama, Claire observed sadly—and felt the tears begin to threaten as they always did when she let herself think of her mother.

'Please...' she murmured a little thickly to the man who was standing silently by. 'I need to hold her—can you get her for me?'

Common sense told her not to attempt to bend down there and scoop Melanie up for herself.

'Of course,' he said, and with an economy of movement he bent to lift the baby, straightened and turned towards Claire—only to pause indecisively.

'How will you do this?' he asked, frowning over the problem. 'You don't want to put any stress on your bruised rib-cage.'

Looking around her, Claire decided it was probably best to ease herself into one of the kitchen chairs; at least then she could use the tabletop as an aid to take some of the baby's weight.

A moment after she had settled herself, Melanie arrived in the crook of her arm, and, resting it on the table, Claire released a long, soft, breathy sigh, then lowered her face to the baby's sweet-smelling cheek.

If anyone, having witnessed this moment, could still wonder if she really loved this baby, then they would have had to be blind.

Andreas Markopoulou wasn't blind. But he was moved in a way that would have shocked Claire if she'd happened to glance at him.

Angry was the word. Harshly, coldly—frighteningly angry.

'Ah, you come at last.' Lefka suddenly appeared from another room just off the kitchen, the sound of her heavily accented voice bringing Claire's head up. Looking at Claire with Melanie, the housekeeper smiled warmly. 'You love this baby,' she said, not asking the question but simply stating a fact. 'Good,' she nodded. 'For this baby is an angel. She has stolen my heart.'

Claire had a feeling that she meant it, too; her dark eyes definitely had a love-struck look about them.

'But she will not be happy with me if I do not feed her the bottle soon. So you will show me, please—what to do? My daughter Althea will hold the child.'

By the time Claire had escaped from the kitchen, as reassured as ever anyone could be that Melanie was in safe and loving hands, she had come to a decision.

Going in search of her host, she found him sitting behind his desk, his fingers flying across the laptop keyboard while he talked on the telephone at the same time.

By now, it had gone truly dark outside, and the dark red velvet curtains hanging behind him had been closed, the room softly lit by several intelligently placed table lamps that didn't try to fight against the inviting glow of the fire.

As he glanced up and saw Claire standing there, she saw that the whole effect had softened and enriched his

Mediterranean skin tone, helping to smooth out the harsher angles to his lean-boned face so he looked younger somehow—much less intimidating than he had started to appear to her.

'I'll stay here,' she announced.

CHAPTER THREE

'FOR Melanie's sake,' she added, knowing she sounded surly, but then, she was resenting her own climb-down so her voice was projecting that.

But the last hour spent with Melanie had turned out to be a tough lesson in how little she was able to do for the baby in her present state. And, although witnessing the way Lefka and her daughter Althea had been efficient and gentle and unendingly caring as they saw to her sister had been the main factor that had brought about her decision, her stubborn soul found it a bitter pill to take.

So Claire stood in stiff silence, watching those thoughtful eyes study her, and waited with gritted teeth for him to ask her why she had changed her mind.

Yet he didn't do that. All he did was nod his dark head in mute acceptance of her decision.

A diplomat, she thought, mocking his restraint.

'I will show you to your room, then,' he said, coming gracefully to his feet.

'No need.' She shook her head. 'Althea is going to do that. But I do need some things from my flat,' she then added. 'Fresh clothes and—things,' she explained, feeling a faint flush working its way into her cheeks when she saw the way his gaze dropped automatically to the disreputable state of the 'things' she was presently wearing.

In truth, she felt a bit like a bag lady that had been brought in off the street and allowed to experience how the other half lived.

'If you give Althea a list of your requirements, I will send her with her father to collect them.'

Definitely the diplomat, she reiterated silently as she picked up on his carefully neutralised tone.

'Thank you,' she murmured politely. Then, 'Her father?' she questioned, realising what he had just said.

'Nikos, my chauffeur,' he nodded, coming around his desk. 'They have the top floor to this house as a self-contained apartment.'

As he talked he had been walking smoothly towards her, and the closer he came, the more her nerve-ends began to flutter. Why, she wasn't sure. Then he came to a stop in front of her and reached out to gently cup her chin, arrogantly lifting it so she had to look at him—and she knew exactly why her nerve-ends became agitated whenever he came too close.

Her flesh liked to feel his flesh against it, and that implied a sexual attraction that she just did not want to acknowledge.

'Stop being afraid of me,' he commanded, obviously seeing something flash in her guarded blue eyes.

'I'm not.' She denied the charge, but pulled away from his touch anyway.

Sighing slightly, he turned away from her, but not before she had glimpsed a hint of irritation with her. 'I have the keys to your home,' he announced, as cool and flat as calm waters. And, at her soft gasp of surprise because she hadn't given a single thought as to where her keys were, he turned back again, to flick her with one of his unfathomable looks. 'As you were being transferred into the ambulance, I instructed Nikos to make your flat safe and lock up,' he explained.

'Then if you have my keys,' she shot at him sarcastically, 'I'm surprised you didn't have the whole place transferred here while I couldn't stop you!'

She was referring to the very unpalatable fact that her sister seemed to have acquired a complete new wardrobe of clothes—plus just about every gadget ever invented to make a mother's life an easier one!

To her amazement he stiffened up as if she had just hit him! 'I would not be so ill-mannered as to remove anything from your home without your permission!' he informed her haughtily. 'It would be tantamount to stealing!'

'Yet you felt no qualms about stealing me!' Claire shot back.

Irritation really showed on his hard face now. 'I—stole *both* of you.' He made that fine but seemingly important distinction. 'For your own good, since we both know you cannot manage without my help. Now, can we drop this—conversation?' he went on impatiently. 'It is serving no useful purpose—and I have more important work to do!'

Stung by his tone and being made to feel like an awkward child who had just been severely reprimanded by an adult, Claire turned without another word and reached for the door.

'Don't…' The gruff voice sounded too close to her ear.

'Don't what?' she mumbled, the too ready tears not far away.

He didn't reply; instead he reached around her with his arm, his hand appearing in front of her misted vision as it closed over her own hand and gently prised it free of the door handle. Just as gently, he turned her round to face him and Claire found herself looking at the blurred bulk of his white-shirted chest once again.

She heard him sigh, and wished she could stop being so pathetic! It was humiliating to keep wanting to cry like this! 'This isn't going to work,' she choked.

'Just because we fight,' he replied, his deep voice completely wiped clean of all hint of anger, 'it does not mean that we cannot get along with each other. It simply shows that we are two very strong-willed people who both like to win in an argument.'

It seemed to Claire that he had been winning every single battle they'd fought today—which didn't say much for her own strength of will.

'Well, try not to be so arrogant,' she advised, firmly push-

ing herself away from him. 'And maybe we will get through
this without killing each other.'

With that she turned back to the door, opened it and
walked away, rather pleased for grabbing the last word for a
change—and surprised that he'd let her have it without cutting the legs out from under her.

Althea showed her to a rather elegant bedroom suite decorated and furnished in a tasteful range of soft blues through
to watery greens. There was a large white *en-suite* bathroom
that seemed to have been stocked with just about every re-
quirement anyone could possibly look for, plus a cavernous
walk-in dressing room lined with custom-designed shelves
and hanging space.

Her pathetically few items of clothing were going to look
really great in here, Claire thought ruefully, turning her attention back to the main bedroom and looking around her to
decide where she was going to place Melanie's crib when it
arrived.

Then she stopped, realising suddenly that she wasn't going
to be able to have Melanie in here with her! Not unless
Althea or her mother came along with the baby—for how
was she supposed to deal with nights feeds when she couldn't
even manage to fix a teat into a bottle, never mind everything
else?

'Where is Melanie going to sleep?' she asked Althea, who
was waiting for her to compose the list of things she needed
from her flat.

And even the writing of a simple list was going to be
completely beyond her, she realised next. She was going to
have to dictate it to Althea.

Softly spoken, gentle, introverted and shy, Althea answered carefully, 'Mamma suggests, if you agree to it, that
perhaps the little one would be best sleeping next to my bed?'

Which placed not just a room between her and Melanie—
but a whole wretched floor. It hit her hard, that. It had her

standing there gazing helplessly around her, feeling a bit like a boat that had lost its rudder.

The list didn't take very long to dictate. After all, what did Claire need here but a few changes of clothes and the odd personal item? But it was only as Althea left to go and find her father that another thought suddenly struck her, bringing with it a rather ugly clutch of shame at the knowledge that Althea, who was used to living like—this, was going to walk into her shabby little flat and see what Claire and Melanie were more used to.

And pride, Claire Stenson, is a very poor companion! She immediately scolded herself for allowing it to encroach. Hadn't she already learned that salutary little lesson years ago when she and her mother had lost everything—even so-called lifelong friends *and* most of the clothes off their backs?

With that stern reminder, her chin came up, and she turned her attention to something much more important. Namely, needing to use the bathroom quite urgently. Whereby she spent the next ten minutes encountering a whole new set of obstacles that took some trouble to overcome.

She would have liked to fill the bath with hot, fragrant water and lie down in it for ever, but that was so much out of the question that she didn't even bother to do much more than *think* how wonderful it would be. But a shower was a different proposition, she mused, with a thoughtful look at the clear glass cubicle over in the corner...

Spying a long white terry-towelling robe hanging behind the bathroom door made her mind up for her. And with a sudden determination that eventually turned into a panting frustration she struggled out of her dirty clothes.

She only hoped that Althea wasn't long, because there was no way she was putting those clothes back on her body, she decided as she stood there, naked, giving the small pile in the corner of the bathroom a distasteful glare before turning away from it.

Which was when she caught a glimpse of herself in the full-length mirror that was fixed to one of the tiled walls, and all normal thought processes stalled for the moment as dismay completely froze her.

She looked as if someone had given her a good beating. The cut at her temple was pretty minor but the lump that had formed beneath it was distorting the shape of her face! And the bruising on the left-hand side of her lower ribcage had already begun to turn an ugly back and blue.

But that wasn't all of it, she noted woefully. Not nearly all of it. Though the rest was purely personal. A painfully personal view of herself as the man downstairs must have been seeing her each time those dark eyes had settled on her, she realised with a small shudder.

How much weight had she actually lost? she asked herself as she stood there feeling the shock of self-awareness ricochet through her for the first time since her mother had died.

Two months ago she'd had a nice figure—even if she did say so herself! Slender and sleek, not thin and bony! Even her breasts...these small, pointed breasts had absolutely no fullness left in them!

And her hair... Her good hand went up to touch her lank, lifeless hair where it hung around her pale and sadly hollowed-out face.

What had she been doing to herself? Where had she gone? She used to be happy, bright, always smiling, with hair and skin that glowed with health, and a well cared for, athletic body. Not this thin, lank, dull-eyed person who looked as if she'd been kicked black and blue.

She was suddenly filled with an almost overwhelming urge to toss herself in the corner of the bathroom where her ruined clothes lay discarded!

Yet, surprisingly, seeing a vivid picture of herself, sitting there slumped in the corner along with her torn shirt and dirty jeans, was so comical that she laughed.

By the time she had managed to have a shower *and* shampoo her hair whilst keeping her plaster-cast dry by winding her arm around the outside of the cubical wall whilst the other hand did all the work, she emerged from the steamy confines refreshed, smelling sweet, and feeling generally a whole lot better all round. Mainly, she suspected, because she'd managed to do it all for herself without having to ask for any help.

Encouraged by her own success and thinking on her feet now, she decided to let the terry bathrobe do the job of soaking up the excess moisture from her skin so she didn't have to jar her bruises by attempting to dry herself with a towel. In fact, the only task that defeated her was knotting the robe belt around her middle. And that was such a minor thing after all the other obstacles she had so successfully negotiated that she thought nothing more about it as she walked back into the bedroom, dabbing a towel at her damp hair—only to stop dead in her tracks.

'Oh!' The stifled exclamation of surprise left her throat like a sigh, yet he heard it, and it brought him twisting on his heel to face her. Then, for a few short, thickening moments, neither of them moved again.

It's like having time stand still, Claire thought as she stared at his lean, dark face and felt the strangest sensation wash over her—like a sharp implement being drawn down her backbone, setting off a sensory chain reaction that had her whole system tingling.

Then he spoke. 'For goodness' sake,' he bit out. 'Do you have to look so disturbed that you find me here? I have not come to ravish you—though it may be prudent for you to— do something about the robe,' he suggested, with a grim flick of the hand that sent her wide eyes jerking downwards.

In an agony of dismay she dropped the towel so she could whip the two sides of the robe together across her naked front, then clamped them there with her plastered wrist.

'Have you never heard of knocking?' she choked, almost suffocating in her own embarrassment.

'I did knock,' he replied. 'But when I received no answer I let myself in, believing you may well be sleeping.'

'Which makes it all right, does it?' She flashed him a hot, resentful glance. 'You see nothing wrong in coming into a guest's bedroom while she sleeps in blissful ignorance of your presence?'

If she said all of that to hit back at him for embarrassing her, it didn't work. All he did was throw up his arrogant head and glare at her as if he was waiting for *her* to apologise for *his* intrusion!

Then he let out an impatient sigh. 'This is all so unnecessarily foolish,' he muttered, and began striding towards her with the kind of purpose that had Claire backing warily.

'Stop it!' he hissed, reaching down to grab hold of the two ends of the robe belt that were hanging at either side of her. With a firm yank he brought her to a standstill, then proceeded to tower over her like some avenging dark angel.

He was angry, she could see that. But there was something else going on behind that hard, tight expression that seriously disturbed her—though at that moment she wasn't sure why.

Then he bent towards her. He's going to kiss me! she thought wildly, and gasped out some kind of shaky little protest as her heart gave a painful thump against her ribs then began palpitating madly when panic erupted in a roaring mad rush that set her brain spinning.

What he actually did do was knot her robe belt around her middle. It was like being on a helter-skelter ride of out-of-control emotion. Instead of feeling high as a kite on panic, she suddenly felt dizzy with the effects of a sinking relief.

Then he kissed her.

And after everything else that had gone before it she had nothing—nothing left to fight him with. The sense of relief had relaxed all the tension out of her, so he caught her undefended, his mouth crushing hers with a ruthless precision that literally shocked her breathless.

Warm, smooth, very knowledgeable lips fused warmly

with hers. Blue eyes wide open with shock and staring, she found herself looking straight down into the black abyss of his. The rest of her followed, free-falling into that terrible darkness without the means to stop herself.

Then he was gone. As abruptly as he had made the contact, he withdrew it.

'Now be afraid,' he grimly invited, and while she stood there just staring at him with huge blank blue eyes he turned on his heel and strode off to the other side of the room.

In the sizzling taut silence which followed she could have heard a pin drop on the thick carpet beneath her bare feet. She was too stunned to speak and he was obviously still too angry.

For anger it had been that had made him kiss her like that; she wasn't so punch-drunk as not to have recognised that. It had been a kiss to punish, not a kiss to frighten. He had already warned her several times today that he reacted badly to challenge.

Well, she had just received personal experience of that bad reaction, Claire acknowledged. 'If you ever do that again, I will scratch your eyes out,' she informed him shakily.

'Before or after you expose your body to me?'

He was such a merciless devil! If her legs hadn't felt so shaky she would have gone over there and scratched his eyes out anyway!

Then she remembered what it had felt like to fall into them, and shivered, the will to fight shrivelling out of her because she never wanted to risk looking into those eyes like that again.

So instead she began looking around her in a rather dazed effort to remember what she had been doing when she'd discovered him here.

She saw the white towel lying on the deep blue carpet and remembered she had been using it to dry the excess water off her wet hair. Knowing that bending to pick it up again was completely beyond her physical abilities at the moment, she ignored the towel and went over to the dressing table where, earlier, she had spied a hairbrush.

He was standing with his back to her, in front of a polished wood tallboy inside which, Althea had shown her, were housed a television set and a very expensive-looking music system.

The room with everything, she thought sarcastically, and grimaced as she picked up the hairbrush and began drawing it through her damp hair.

'What are you here for anyway?' she asked, needing to break through the silence. 'I presume you did have a reason to come in here?'

He turned, stiff, tense, and supremely remote—like a man sitting alone on the top of a mountain, she thought, and felt a return of her earlier sense of humour at the absurd image.

No apology forthcoming this time, she noted, and the smile actually reached her eyes.

He saw it, didn't like it and frowned, something interestingly like the pompous male equivalent to a blush streaking a hint of colour across his dark cheekbones. Fascinated by that, Claire turned more fully to face him so she could see how he was going to deal with this momentary loss of his precious composure.

Recognising exactly what she was doing and why, he released a heavy sigh. 'How are the ribs?'

Ah, a diversion, she noted. 'Sore,' she replied, telling the blunt truth of it.

'And the wrist?'

'Agony,' she grimaced.

'Then maybe I did the right thing coming in here to bring you—these...' He was holding up a small bottle of what had to be tablets. 'Pain-killers,' he explained. 'Issued by the hospital. I forgot I had them.'

Half turning, he placed the bottle on the top of the tallboy. Then he turned back to Claire. 'Where is your sling?'

Glancing down to where her plastered wrist was hanging

heavily at her side, 'I must have left it in the bathroom,' she replied, putting down the hairbrush so she could use her hand to lift the cast into a more comfortable position resting against her middle.

Without another word he strode off, his composure intact now, and his arrogance along with it, she observed as she watched him disappear into the bathroom then come out again carrying the modern version of a sling in his hand.

About to approach her, he paused, thought twice about it, then—sardonically—requested, 'May I?'

Her wry half nod gave her permission and he came forward. By then she had moved to ease herself into a sitting position on the edge of the dressing table, so he really towered over her this time as he coolly looped the sling-belt over her head then gently took hold of her plastered wrist.

'You didn't even get it wet,' he remarked.

'I'm a very clever girl,' she answered lightly.

'And sometimes,' he drawled, 'you are very reckless and naïve.'

'How you can make such a sweeping remark about me when you've barely known me for a day is beyond me,' she threw right back. Then she broke the banter to issue a wince and a groan as he gently eased the weighty plaster-cast into its support.

Instantly his eyes flicked upwards to her face, wondrously lustrous curling black lashes coiling away from those dangerous black holes to reveal—not anger, but genuine concern.

'How much pain are you actually in?' he demanded huskily.

A lot, she wanted to say, but tempered the reply to a rueful, 'Some,' that was supposed to have sounded careless but ended up quivering as it left her.

The anger came back then. 'How much and where?' He grimly insisted on a truthful answer.

'All over,' she confessed as all hint of flippancy drained

right out of her and her throat began to thicken with pathetic, weak tears.

On a soft curse, he moved away from her again, going back into the bathroom to return carrying a glass of water. Not even glancing her way, he strode across the room to pick up the pill bottle. Coming back, he handed her the glass of water then shook two small pills into his palm. In grim silence he offered them to her. And in tearful silence she took them and washed them down with the water.

A tear trickled down her cheek. She went to wipe it away with the glass—but he got there before her, his long fingers gently splaying across her damp hair while he smoothed his thumb pad across her cheek.

And the worst of it was, she wanted to lean right into those splayed fingers. She wanted to bury her face in his big hard chest and sob her wretched heart out!

'I can't even stand up!' she confessed despairingly. 'My hip's gone all stiff—and my thigh and my ribs!'

A moment later she was being lifted into his arms and it hurt like blazes but she didn't care.

'I am such a pathetic baby!' she sobbed as he carried her across the room towards the bed.

'You are hurt. You are shocked. You are exhausted,' he responded sternly. 'Which means you are allowed to be pathetic.'

A joke! She laughed, and the tears stopped.

Laying her carefully on the bed, he reached across her and flipped the other side of the king-size duvet over her. His face was still stern, but she found she liked looking at it now.

'How old are you?' she asked curiously.

He paused as he was about to straighten. Looked into pool-deep blue eyes—and offered her a cold little grimace. 'As old as the hills,' he drawled—and stood back. 'Now rest,' he ordered. 'And let the pain-killers do their job. We eat in…' he took a quick glance at the paper-thin gold watch he had wrapped around his hair-peppered wrist '…two hours. By then Althea should be back with your things. So you may get up and join me for dinner downstairs, or you can eat up here. The choice is yours.'

With that he turned and was gone. It was like having the fire go out suddenly, Claire decided with a shiver, then frowned, wondering why she was comparing him to a fire when he was more like a freezer most of the time...

She went downstairs for dinner. Mainly because she didn't want to be a bigger nuisance to these people than she was already being—and because she was desperate to see Melanie, who was being bathed and fed by Lefka while Althea unpacked Claire's clothes then helped her to dress in a fresh pair of jeans and a simple black tee shirt that was loose enough and baggy enough to pull on and off without causing her too much trouble.

Althea showed her into a large drawing room that was nicely decorated in champagne golds and soft greens. Another fire was burning in the grate and the soft sounds of classical music floated soothingly in the air.

Andreas was there, dressed in a fresh pale blue shirt and a pair of steel-grey trousers that sat neatly on his lean waist. But what really surprised her was to find him holding Melanie comfortably at his shoulder.

'You look better,' he remarked, bringing her eyes up from the baby to find him running his gaze over her now shiny gold hair. It had dried on its own while she'd rested and really needed styling, but its own slight kink had saved it from looking a complete fly-away mess.

'I feel it,' she nodded, with a smile that brought his eyes into focus on hers. Whatever it was that was written in those dark depths, Claire suddenly found herself remembering that kiss earlier, and had to break the contact quickly before she embarrassed herself by blushing.

'How has she been?' she then asked anxiously, looking

back at Melanie who looked so tiny against the broad expanse of his chest.

'Like an angel,' he drawled. 'So Lefka informs me. She is smitten,' he confided—then said more softly, 'And I cannot blame her.'

He really meant it, too, Claire realised as she briefly flicked her eyes back to his face to find it softening as he glanced at the baby.

'She is awake. Would you like to hold her?'

'Oh, yes, please...' No one—unless they'd experienced it—could know what it felt like to be separated from the baby she had taken care of single-handedly since their mother had died.

'Perhaps if you sit down on one of the comfortable chairs then you can cradle her in your lap,' he suggested.

Claire didn't need telling twice; walking over to one of the champagne-coloured easy chairs, she sank carefully into its comfort-soft cushions then eagerly accepted the baby.

The moment that Melanie saw Claire's face smiling down on her, her tiny mouth broke into a welcoming smile.

'She knows you,' he said, sounding surprised.

'Of course,' Claire answered. 'I'm her surrogate mother—aren't I, my darling?'

After that she completely forgot about Andreas Markopoulou, who, after a moment or two, lowered himself into the chair opposite them then sat looking on as Claire immersed herself in the sheer pleasure of her mother's baby, talking softly to her while Melanie looked and listened with rapt attention.

Dinner was pleasant. Nothing fancy, just simple but tasty vegetable soup followed by boiled rice and thin slivers of pan-fried chicken that she could easily manage to eat by only using her fork.

Refusing the deep red full-blooded wine he was drinking with his meal, she asked for water instead. And they talked quietly. Well, she talked—Claire made the wry distinction—

while he encouraged her with strategically placed questions that resulted in her whole life to date getting aired at that dinner table.

When she eventually sat back, talked-out and replete, having refused any dessert to finish her meal, she made herself ask the question that had been troubling her on and off throughout the whole day.

Only one day? She paused to consider this with a small start of surprise. It was beginning to feel as if she'd spent a whole lifetime here with this strangely attentive, very intriguing and enigmatic man.

'Why did you send my aunt away?' she asked him.

He sat back in his own chair to idly finger his wineglass while he studied her face through faintly narrowed eyes.

'She was never very close to you or your mother, was she?' he said, frustratingly blocking the question with a question.

Still, Claire answered it. 'They never got on,' she admitted with a shrug. 'My mother was…' She stopped, her soft mouth twisting slightly because what she was going to say sounded as if she was being critical of a mother she'd adored—when in actual fact it wasn't a criticism but a flat statement of fact. 'A bit frivolous.' She made herself say it. 'Aunt Laura was the older sister. Much tougher and…less pretty,' she added with wry honesty.

'People liked to spoil my mother.' Even I did, she thought, glancing at those slightly narrowed, intent black eyes then away again quickly. 'Aunt Laura would have bitten their heads off for trying the same thing with her,' she went on. 'She's a staunch feminist with a good business brain and she likes to use it.'

He nodded in agreement and once again Claire felt herself being subtly encouraged to continue. 'She has no time for— sentimentality.' Claire thought that described her aunt best. 'Her philosophy is that if something goes wrong you either fix it or throw it away and start from scratch again,' she explained sadly.

'And which category do you and Melanie come under?'

'She wants me to have Melanie adopted,' she replied, her expression turning cynical. 'So you tell me because I still haven't decided whether that particular solution is supposed to be fixing us or throwing us out.'

'Which means,' he concluded, 'that you also have not decided whether to take her advice or not.'

Shrewd devil, Claire thought bitterly, and rose tensely to her feet as the rotten truth in that statement hit sharply home. 'Why don't you try answering my question for a change?' she flashed back in sheer bloody reaction. 'And tell me why you sent her away when it has to be obvious that we needed her here right now!'

'I don't need to answer the question,' he replied, super-calm in the face of her sudden hostility. 'For you have just answered it for yourself.'

'What's that supposed to mean?' she demanded frowningly, not understanding what he was getting at.

He didn't seem inclined to explain it either, she observed as he sat there, eyes hooded, face grim while he stared fixedly at his wineglass as if he was weighing up his options.

But—what options? Claire wondered in despairing confusion. She didn't even know why she knew what he was doing! Yet the suggestion stuck while she stood there simmering with frustration and anger, waiting for him to make up his mind.

Then he announced, 'I have a proposition to put to you,' and got to his feet, obviously having made that decision! 'But we will go through to my study before I say any more. For we require privacy and it cannot be guaranteed here when Lefka or Althea could walk in at any moment.'

With that he turned and strode off, obviously expecting Claire to follow him. She did so, frowning and tense again—

very tense as every suspicious thought she'd had about this man and his motives came rushing back.

By the time Claire arrived at the study door he was already standing across the room where a tray of bottles stood on an antique oak sideboard.

'Please shut the door behind you,' he instructed without turning.

Doing as he said, she watched in silence as he selected, uncapped and poured a rather large measure of a dark golden spirit into a squat crystal tumbler.

Clearly, he needed something more fortifying than wine before he put his proposition to her! she noted, and felt her wary tension move up another couple of notches as she waited for him to speak.

'I sent your aunt out of the country on business today,' he began quite suddenly, 'because I decided to get her about as far away from you as I could possibly manage.'

Claire gave a surprised start. 'But—why?' she gasped. 'Why would you want to do that?'

He didn't answer immediately; instead the glass went to his mouth so he could sip at the spirit, gathering tension all around them as it did so.

It was odd—that tension—full of a tingling sense of dark foreboding that even he seemed affected by. As Claire stood there by the door with her wary eyes fixed on his hard, lean face, she gained the strong impression that, despite the decision he seemed to have come to in the dining room, he was still heavily involved in a rather uncharacteristic struggle with himself.

'I have a—personal problem that is threatening to cause me a certain amount of—embarrassment,' he said suddenly. 'I do have a workable solution, however,' he added, glancing back at his glass and tipping it slightly so the golden liquid clung to the sides. 'But it requires a wife and a child to succeed. Meeting you today,' he went on levelly, 'seeing where you live and, more importantly, how you live—it occurred to me that you may well be the ideal candidate for the position...'

'What position?' Claire asked, utterly lost as to what he was getting at.

He grimaced into his glass—she presumed because she was forcing him into being more explicit about what he was talking about.

'As my wife,' he enlightened her. Then, when she still continued to stand there blank-faced and frowning in bewilderment, he lifted his eyes until they fixed sardonically on hers and said, 'I am asking you to marry me, Claire...'

CHAPTER FOUR

CLAIRE released a gasp in stunned disbelief. 'You want to *marry me*?' she repeated.

Then, almost instantly, she decided, No, I've heard him wrong, and laughed—or rather emitted a nervous little giggle that she regretted as soon as it left her lips because the effect it had on him made her feel cruel, as his lean face closed up as tight as a drum.

He's actually serious! she realised. She felt her legs threaten to collapse beneath her and had to move over to one of the dark red recliners and lower herself carefully into it.

'Please do not misunderstand me,' he said, suddenly standing high on his mountain of dignity again. 'I am not suggesting an intimate relationship. Just a—marriage of convenience if you like. Where we will maintain an appearance of intimacy. But that is all...'

No intimacy, she repeated to herself, and as quickly as that her eyes went blank as her imagination shot off to a place where she'd stared into this man's eyes while his mouth had been fused very *intimately* with her own.

'I will, of course, ensure that the—arrangement is a beneficial one for you,' he coldly continued. 'The advantages in being the wife of a very wealthy man do, I think, speak for themselves. And it need not be a lifetime thing—although I will have to insist that I become Melanie's legal father or it will not work.'

'What won't work?' she questioned helplessly.

But he gave a shake of his dark head. 'I can only reveal that if I gain your agreement,' he said. 'But in her becoming my legal daughter,' he went on as if she hadn't made the interruption, 'I will be assuring Melanie's future—which can only be a good thing for her, since she will also become my sole heir. And if and when you decide that it is time for you to leave me so you can get on with your own life you will not go empty-handed.'

Claire's mind was starting to scramble. She was sure that what he was actually saying here, in a carefully veiled way, was that he wanted Melanie, but if Claire had to come along with her, then he was prepared to agree to that.

'I think you're crazy,' she told him.

He grimaced, but didn't argue the point.

'You don't even know me!'

This time it was a shrug. 'I am a man who has always relied on my first impression of people—and I like you, Claire,' he said, as if that should mean something special to her. 'I even admire you for the way you have been coping on your own with a child and little to no help from anyone.'

'I do have help!' she cried, her hackles rising at his too accurate reading of her.

'Do you mean—this kind of help?' he asked, and from his trouser pocket he withdrew a wad of bank notes.

As she stared at them as if she had never so much as laid eyes on paper money before, it took a few moments for it to sink in what he was actually showing her.

Her eyes shot to his. 'Is that the money Aunt Laura left for me today?'

'You dropped it on the floor in your flat when you fainted,' he explained. 'I picked it up and placed it in my pocket for safekeeping. I counted it earlier; there is exactly one hundred pounds here,' he informed her grimly. 'Knowing the dire straits of your circumstances, that you owe at least four times that amount on your rent *and* being fully aware that you also have to exist somehow, your aunt condescended to leave you a paltry one hundred pounds.'

To Claire, who had nothing, one hundred pounds was an absolute fortune! But it obviously wasn't to this man. For the way he tossed the money aside made his disgust more than clear.

'In effect, what she was doing,' he went on, remorseless in his determination to get his own point across, 'was wearing you down so that you would begin to look on her proposal more favourably. I got that much out of her while you were half comatose,' he inserted tightly. 'And she was trying her best to explain to me why her only relatives were living in that kind of squalor.'

Claire closed her eyes, the word 'squalor' cutting right to the heart of her.

'You already knew about her suggestion before I told you,' she breathed, feeling the sharp sting of one that had been well and truly tricked by his quiet interest in her during dinner.

Maybe he saw it. 'I am sorry if that offends you,' he said. 'But it is important here that you keep your mind focused on what is best for you and Melanie. And if it has come down to a choice between having the child adopted and my offer, then I think mine is your better option.'

'But then you would, wouldn't you?' Claire pointed out, and came stiffly to her feet. 'Now I want my baby and I want to go home,' she informed him with enough ice-cold intent to match any he could dish out.

It made his face snap with irritation. 'Don't be foolish!' he rasped. 'That is no solution and only promises you more misery!'

I'm miserable now, Claire thought unhappily. 'I thought you were kind!' she burst out, blue eyes bright with a pained disillusionment. 'I thought you genuinely cared about what had happened to me! When all the time while you've been shadowing me around today you've been plotting this!'

Her voice rose on a clutch of hurt. He winced at the sound of it. 'I *am* kind!' he growled, looking faintly uncomfortable with his own role here.

Claire's thick huff of scorn made his eyes flash warningly,

then, with a grimace, he seemed to be allowing her the right to be scornful.

'I can be kind,' he amended huskily, scraped an impatient set of long fingers through his hair, then even amended the amendment. 'I *will* be kind,' he declared in a voice that made it a promise.

Still, it held no sway with Claire. 'Thank you for the offer but no, thank you,' she refused, moving stiffly towards the door.

'Before you walk through that door, Miss Stenson, don't you think you should take a moment to consider what your decision is going to mean to your sister...?'

Smooth as silk, his voice barely revealing an inflection, his words still had her steps faltering and growing still, the fine quiver touching her soft mouth sign enough that, just like her aunt, he had managed to find the right button to press without having to look very hard for it.

'But—why?' she cried, lifting perplexed blue eyes to his deadly ruthless face. 'If you feel such a strong need to will your possessions to someone, then why not get a family of your own?'

It didn't make sense—none of it did. Neither did the way he suddenly stiffened up as if he'd been shot. 'I will never marry again,' he said. 'Not in the way you are suggesting anyway.'

'You've been married before?'

'Yes. Sofia—died six years ago.' The confirmation was coldly blunt.

'Oh...I'm so sorry,' Claire murmured, her expression immediately softening into sympathy.

His did the opposite. 'I have no wish to discuss it,' he clipped, and the way he said it was enough to stop Claire from daring to ask any more questions.

But she was curious. Suddenly very curious about the woman he had lost whom he must have loved very deeply if he never wanted to marry again. Not for real, anyway, she dryly tagged onto that.

'There are other ways these days to get children without having to commit yourself to marriage, you know,' she pointed out gently. 'Medical science has become quite clever in that respect.'

'I am Greek,' he replied as if that explained everything. And he didn't elaborate. Instead he pulled everything back to the main issue. 'I want you to consider very carefully what you will be gaining if you agree to marry me. For you will get to bring up your mother's child in the kind of luxury most people only dream of.'

Humility is not one of his strongest points, Claire made wry note.

'Think of it,' he urged. 'No more living from hand to mouth. No more having to go without so you can ensure that the child is clothed and fed. No worrying where the next week's rent is coming from. Instead,' he concluded, listing the advantages of his so-called proposal in much the same way her aunt had done when talking about Melanie's adoption, 'you will receive a generous monthly allowance to do with what you will. And since all our homes will have more than enough paid staff to relieve you of the less enjoyable chores involved in caring for a baby you will have the time and the leisure to enjoy life rather than sacrificing it to your baby sister.'

'I don't see it as a sacrifice.' Her chin came up, blue eyes glittering with indignation. 'And I resent the implication that I may do.'

'My apologies,' he retracted instantly. 'It was not my intention to offend.'

No, Claire could see it wasn't. This was just too important to him to want to risk offending her—which immediately brought about her next question. 'Why does it mean so much to you to get me? To get Melanie?' she asked. 'You could walk out of here right now and simply pick up a dozen women with children who could fill this role just as well as we can!'

'But I want you both,' he stated simply. 'Why don't you ask yourself why it is that you are so afraid of what I am offering you?'

'Because it feels wrong,' she replied, then added honestly, 'And I'm too young for this role.'

'Or is it me who is too old?'

He's the type who will never be old. 'How old is that exactly? And don't give me the flippant answer I got the last time I asked you that question,' she warned. 'Because I'm serious. If you want me to consider your proposition I need to know.'

'Thirty-six,' he replied, and grimaced at her astonished expression.

She gave a small sigh, then turned to lean back against the closed door. 'This is crazy,' she muttered, thinking out loud. But what was even crazier was the knowledge that she was beginning to waver.

No more worries, she told herself. No more living from day to day in a place she hated with no prospect of ever getting something better—if you didn't count what was being offered here. Then there was Melanie to consider. Melanie, who would want for nothing for the rest of her life, if his sincerity was to be believed.

It was all very seductive, she mused, lifting her hand to gently rub at the bump on her temple as her head began to ache.

He saw the gesture and was instantly all concern. 'It is clear that you have had enough for one day,' he murmured huskily. 'Let us leave this for now, and come back to it tomorrow when you are feeling more rested.'

He was right—and she had taken enough, Claire acknowledged wearily. But she said, 'No.' She shook her head. 'I won't sleep for worrying about all of this unless we resolve it now.'

She lifted tired, bruised, anxious eyes to his. 'Will you please tell me *why* you need a ready-made wife and baby?' she begged.

There was a pause, then he asked smoothly, 'Are you telling me you are going to accept my proposition?'

He isn't going to give a single inch to me, she noted. 'I'm thinking about it,' she replied.

'Then while you think I will think about telling you why I want you to marry me.'

Cat and mouse. Cut and thrust. 'Then goodnight,' she said, and turned back to the door.

'I like the hair, by the way...'

Her hair? Her hand went up, self-conscious fingertips lightly touching the ends of a fine silk tendril.

'It is such a wonderful colour...'

'Thank you,' she murmured, blushing slightly at the unexpected compliment.

'Neither blonde nor red,' he softly observed. 'But a rather fascinating mixture of the two... I wonder what colour it will go with a Greek sunset pouring all over it?'

'I've never been to Greece,' Claire sighed, heard the wistful note in her voice and knew that he must be able to hear it too.

'You'll love it,' he promised as he walked towards her. 'Sizzling hot days and delightfully warm nights. Though you will have to protect your fine white skin from the sun,' he warned. 'But Melanie's skin will love it. Whatever nationality her father was, he gifted her with the rich olive skin of a true Mediterranean.'

'Spanish,' Claire inserted. 'Her father was Spanish.' Then a sudden thought had her glancing sharply at him. 'Is that why you want her?' she asked. 'Because she has the right skin tone to be passed off as your daughter?'

But he shook his dark head. He was standing so close to her now that she could actually see the wry humour hovering in his dark eyes. 'With a golden-haired, pale-skinned English wife, my child could have been blessed with her colouring,' he pointed out.

Looking away again, Claire frowned, the conundrum behind his reason for wanting them beginning to irritate her like an itch she couldn't quite reach. 'Well...' She gave a small shrug of one narrow shoulder as if the itch were situated there, and turned away from him yet again. 'I'll...'

'My family is trying to make me marry again, and produce an heir to my fortune.'

He caved in so suddenly and produced the information that for a moment Claire couldn't believe that he'd actually done it! It went so against what she'd believed she'd already learned about his calculating nature!

'They have my proposed bride already picked out for me,' he went on. 'And the pressure is mounting because my grandmother is ill. She wants to hold her great-grandchild before she dies. And since I am the only grandson she has it is up to me to grant her that wish.'

'How ill?' Claire asked gently.

'Very.' The shadowy outline of his mouth flicked out that grim brief smile again. 'She is ninety-two years old and has just suffered her second stroke. She does not have long left on this earth.'

And he loves her and is going to miss her dreadfully, Claire realised as she saw a darkness come down over those unfathomable eyes, and felt her heart give a pinch of well understood sympathy.

'I don't have time to play around with alternatives,' he admitted. 'So your arrival in my life was a piece of good fortune I could not afford to dismiss. As I have told you before, I respond to my instincts. And my instincts tell me that we three could make a good team.' His eyes flicked up, clashed with her eyes and Claire suddenly felt as if she were falling again. 'When my grandmother is no longer here to see it happen, you can leave whenever you are ready to...'

No hearts compromised, no feelings touched. 'More like a temporary job, in fact.'

'For you, yes,' he agreed, with a small shrug. 'But not for Melanie...' he made firmly clear. 'Melanie will be my daughter in every way I can make it so. I want her, Claire,' he added huskily. 'I *need* her.'

'But will you *love* her?' she challenged.

'As my own and all my life,' he vowed. And he meant it; Claire could see that in the fierce glow of a powerful intent that suddenly lit his eyes.

I wish somebody wanted me like that, she found herself thinking wistfully. 'And when I decide to go—what happens to Melanie?'

'She goes with you,' he said—but only after a hesitation that hit a warning button inside her head. 'So long as you will promise to respect my rights as her legal father, we will agree on an affable arrangement which will suit both of our needs where she is concerned. For Melanie's sake alone, it has to be her best chance in life, don't you think?'

For Melanie's sake, Claire repeated silently, knowing exactly where she had heard those words before, and not liking the sensation that trickled down her spine at the connection.

But, despite that nasty sensation, one important thing she did know for sure was that, having once lived in privileged comfort herself—though not anywhere near the style he was offering Melanie here—and having gained tough experience at the poorer end of the scale, Claire knew which end of that scale she preferred to be.

'I'll do it,' she heard herself say. 'For Melanie's sake.'

And only wondered as she did so whether this hadn't been a case of him caving in first, but simply a very astute man knowing exactly when to play his final card.

'Thank you,' he murmured. 'I will promise you, Claire, that you will never have cause to regret this decision.'

But she was already regretting it as early as the next morning when she came down the stairs ready to tell him that she had changed her mind.

At which point she discovered that Andreas Markopoulou had pulled yet another tactical move on her, by going abroad on business for the next frustratingly long week.

Melanie, in the meantime, was beginning to bloom with all the tender loving care both Lefka and Althea were ladling upon her. Claire didn't hear her cry once!

Secretly she found it hurtful. For, under Claire's exclusive care, the little girl had hardly ever *stopped* crying since their mother had died.

Then, most hurtful of all, was the way her aunt hadn't once bothered to get in touch with her. Whether that was her aunt's own indifference or Andreas Markopoulou's doing she didn't know. But, knowing Aunt Laura as well as she did, if she'd wanted to contact Claire then she would have done, no matter what her big tycoon boss might say.

But, as the week slid by, at least her body began to heal; the bump on her temple disappeared altogether and her bruises began to fade. Even her hurt feelings had given way to a dull acceptance—along with her acceptance that she could no more take Melanie away from what she was receiving here than sprout wings and fly.

So it was that she was sitting in the solarium at the back of the house, gently pushing Melanie's pram to and fro to rock the baby to sleep, when a voice murmured to one side of her, 'You look a lot better...'

She didn't turn to look at him, but her hand stopped rocking the baby carriage. And her heart gave an excited leap that left her feeling tense and shaky.

Still, at least her voice was steady when she answered coolly, 'A week is a long time.'

'Ah...' He came forward, his footsteps sounding on the quarry-tiled floor beneath his feet. 'I thought it best to leave you alone to—come to terms with your decision.'

So he was admitting to a retreat, she noted, and was oddly

pacified by that—then even more so when he paused at the pram to bend down and inspect Melanie.

'She's asleep,' he whispered. But it was the way he stroked a gentle finger over the baby's cheek in much the same way that Claire did that touched a warm spot inside her.

Then, pulling up one of the other cane chairs, he sat down beside her. 'How is the wrist?' he enquired.

'Better,' she told him.

'And the ribs?'

'They don't hurt when I laugh any more,' she replied with a grin she turned to offer directly to him.

Then wished she hadn't when her heart gave that funny leap again, making the tiny muscles deep in her stomach coil up in reaction. He looked lean and dark and sun-kissed, as if he'd just stepped off a plane from a place where the weather had been a lot pleasanter than it had been here in England.

She felt a tingling urge to reach out and touch his face just to feel if it was as warm as it appeared to be. 'Where have you been?' she asked instead, leaving the less tactile medium of words to assuage her curiosity.

'You sound like a wife,' he mocked, his dark eyes flickering slightly as he scanned her face where even Claire had noticed the stray-waif look was beginning to fade.

'Not yet,' she drawled in answer. 'And for all you know I may have changed my mind.'

'Have you?'

The urge to prolong his agony and lie almost got the better of her, but in the end she said, 'No,' and they were both silent for several minutes. The baby made a snuffling sound and she began rocking the pram again. It was all very—ordinary.

'I've been in Greece,' he announced, answering her earlier question. 'With my grandmother,' he added, and though his tone was level Claire knew instinctively that something was wrong.

'She's worse, isn't she?' she said.

'Fading fast,' he grimaced—then added briskly, 'So I have set her a task to do to keep her mind occupied. She is planning our wedding as we speak.'

Startled, Claire straightened in the chair. 'Our wedding?' she repeated. 'But I thought you wanted to present her with a *fait accompli*!'

'No.' He shook his head. 'That would not have worked quite so successfully as the story I have now fed her.'

'Which is—what?' she demanded, only managing to keep her angry voice down in respect of the sleeping Melanie.

'That you are young and very beautiful...'

Beautiful? Claire stared directly ahead and wondered how he could lie so glibly, because the one thing she wasn't was beautiful! Passably attractive when at her best, she conceded. But nothing more than that.

'I told her that we had shared a—liaison some time last year,' he went on. 'But because of your youth I broke it off, not knowing I was leaving you carrying my child...'

Lie number two, she counted, and began to see for the first time what mire of deceit she was about to fall into.

'But I could not get you out of my mind—which was why I found it so impossible to agree to marry another woman while I still wanted you. So I went to see you,' he explained. 'And as for the rest—' he shrugged '—it tells itself.'

It certainly did, Claire agreed, seeing herself as this tragic young woman who'd fallen for the big handsome Greek tycoon who was, by the sound of it, not far off his dotage.

'Actually,' he said, 'the new slant I have put on our—story—' he used the word dryly '—was done to serve a second purpose...'

Now what? Claire wondered, feeling the fine hairs on the back of her neck begin to prickle warningly.

'For this way you don't have to *like* the fact that you are marrying me,' he explained. 'Being the arrogant dictator that everyone seems to think I am—including you—no one is going to question the idea that you have been—coerced into becoming my wife for the sake of our child. Which also means you get your own bedroom without tongues wagging,' he pointed out. 'While I must—earn your affections again.'

'And thereby ends the tale when I eventually turn my back on you and walk away,' Claire finished for him. 'Not quite the stuff of a romantic novel, is it?' she mocked.

'Life rarely is,' he drawled, sounding suddenly so cold that Claire couldn't believe her ears! With one lightly mocking comment she seemed to have turned him to stone!

Stiffly, he came to his feet. 'We leave for Greece in the morning,' he announced. 'Now I have some work to do. So if you will excuse me…' And, with a curt little bow, he was gone!

What was all that about? Claire found herself wondering in blank bewilderment. And spent the next half an hour trawling over every single word they'd said to each other without coming up with a single thing which could have caused that kind of reaction!

His grandmother: she finally decided to blame it on her. It had to be because he was worried about her.

But deep down inside she somehow knew that wasn't true.

CHAPTER FIVE

THEY flew out to Athens by private charter then transferred to a helicopter for the final leg of the journey. It was all very comfortable, a very trouble-free way to travel in fact.

Claire was impressed—despite not wanting to be, for she still hadn't forgiven Andreas for his sudden coldness the day before.

Melanie was with them, which had surprised her rather. She had expected him to insist that the baby travel with Lefka and her family, who were to close up the London house before catching a later flight. But what really astonished her was the way Andreas took personal responsibility for the baby by seeing to her needs throughout the whole journey.

He was more relaxed than she had ever seen him before. A bit quiet, maybe, but very attentive. So much so that it was a shame that she was still feeling so annoyed with him, because she suspected that he was doing all of this as a way to make up for his bewildering attitude.

Yet he hadn't apologised for it, or explained it. He blew hot and cold on her so swiftly that it seemed to be easier to withdraw and keep herself aloof from him rather than risk having it happen all over again.

'Here, let me help you...' Cradling the baby in one big arm, he offered Claire the steadying strength of the other to help her negotiate the long step down from the helicopter.

With one hand out of action and because she was wearing her only good suit today—a summer-blue silk-linen mix with a fitted jacket and skirt that would not allow her much flexibility in her steps—she needed his help, so she couldn't refuse. But feeling that rock-solid forearm flex beneath her

palm had such a disturbing effect on her that she removed
her hand just as soon as she could do it.

But, worse, she knew that he had sensed her reluctance to
touch him when she saw his mouth tighten as he turned away
to carry Melanie away from the noise of the rotor blades.

Smothering a heavy sigh, Claire followed more slowly,
feeling decidedly at odds with herself and most definitely at
odds with him. She hadn't slept last night for worrying and
fretting about this whole crazy situation. Now she felt tired
and fed up and…

'Oh,' she gasped, coming to a surprised standstill at his
side as she focused at last on her new surroundings.

Set in vast formal gardens, the house stood like a statement
to all that was right in grace and architectural posture. No
one feature had been allowed to dominate. The walls were
painted in the softest cream, the woodwork glossy white, and
the roof was constructed in flat grey slate rather than the
terracotta she would have expected. A first-floor veranda ran
right across the front of the house, casting gentle shade onto
the terrace below, where the palest blue-cushioned wooden
garden furniture waited invitingly.

Over to one side of the house, she could see a large swimming pool shimmering in the afternoon sunshine, and even
spied a second pool under a high domed glass roof attached
to the house itself. If there was a road nearby, she could
neither see nor hear any evidence of it, but a long straight
driveway led off into the distance, lined on either side by tall
cypress trees.

'But this is lovely,' she murmured.

'Praise indeed,' he drawled with cutting sarcasm. 'I was
beginning to think that nothing was going to please you.'

With that he turned his back on her again to walk off
towards the house. With a small grimace, Claire followed,
half allowing him his right to have lost his grasp on all of
that quiet patience he had been doling out to her all day.

He had stepped beneath the shaded end of the terrace before pausing to allow her to catch up with him, his long, lean body making a half turn so he could watch her approach through slightly hooded eyes.

Glancing up and noticing his scrutiny, Claire felt a self-conscious flush of heat wash through her system and quickly looked away again. What was he seeing when he looked at her like that? she wondered. A very big mistake walking towards him?

While she saw a tall, dark, very handsome man with cold black eyes, an unsmiling mouth, and a proud tilt to his chiselled chin that seemed to be trying to tell her something.

Though what that something was, she couldn't have said. The man was a complete enigma.

Hot-cold. Soothe-cut. Approach and retreat. She listed these characteristics of his behaviour with a rueful tilt to her unhappy mouth that seemed to further annoy him. He shifted slightly, looking stiffly tense. The baby woke up with a start and gave a small cry. Claire covered the final few yards in a couple of light dancing steps, her mothering instincts alerted without her even being aware of it.

In the end she wasn't needed. When he glanced down at the baby to find her eyes were open, all the hardness simply melted clean out of him as he lifted a finger to gently touch the baby's small, pointed chin.

But what really took Claire's breath away was the way Melanie's sweet little smile appeared. She knows him already! she realised with a shock.

'Hey,' she complained, peering over his arm so she could look at her sister. 'Those smiles are supposed to belong to me!' she scolded.

As she heard her voice, Melanie's eyes found her face and stuck firmly to it. 'That's better,' Claire grinned, so engrossed in the baby that, far from being disturbed by his closeness, she didn't even notice the way she was leaning against Andreas so she could monopolise the baby's attention.

If she had, she would have realised how still he had gone.

How his hooded eyes had become even more hooded as he settled them on the top of her golden head.

'What a seductive picture,' a beautifully cultured but coldly sarcastic voice intruded. 'I wish I had my camera,' it drawled. 'Then I could capture the image for posterity and you could hang it on the wall as an example of perfect family harmony...'

Two heads came up, one dark, one fair, both faces revealing different expressions. Claire's was startled by this totally unexpected attack; Andreas's was—resigned.

'Desmona...' he greeted smoothly. 'How—nice to see you.'

But it wasn't nice. Desmona wasn't nice and Andreas wasn't being nice. The warm Greek air had suddenly turned chilly and Claire shivered accordingly as she watched the other woman begin walking towards them along the shaded terrace.

She was outstandingly beautiful. A tall and willowy silver-blonde in her early thirties, at a guess, whose silver-blue-silk-encased body glided gracefully as she moved. Money, class and a lifetime of believing herself to be special were reflected in that walk, Claire noted.

Though it was Desmona's eyes that held her thoroughly captivated. If Andreas's eyes could remind her of black ice sometimes, then the silver-grey ones looking at her now could have been set in permafrost, and they intimidated enough to have Claire inching backwards in wary retreat.

The back of her head hit a firmly cushioned shoulder at the same time as an arm curved around her, angling across her rigid back so long, lean brown fingers could rest on her narrow waist. Claire never even considered the idea of moving away from him—not while those silvery eyes were fixed on her anyway.

Was she family? Did she live here? she wondered curiously.

I hope not, she prayed, with a small shudder.

'This, Claire,' Andreas informed her levelly, 'is my sister-in-law Desmona Markopoulou...'

Sister-in-law? With a small start, she flashed him a frowning glance. She was sure he had told her that he was the only grandson.

'*Widowed* sister-in-law.' It was Desmona herself who unwittingly cleared the puzzle as she came to a smooth stop just in front of them. But Claire didn't even like the way she said that.

'May I be the first to welcome you to your new home?' Desmona murmured graciously.

'Thank you,' Claire politely replied.

She was offered a long-fingered, very slender white hand. Claire's own palm began to tingle in anticipation of having to brush against the other woman's satin-smooth skin.

Then the need to touch each other at all was suddenly saved when Claire remembered belatedly that her right hand was in a sling—at about the same moment that Desmona noticed it.

'Oh, you are injured,' she remarked. Her English was superb, spoken with an accent that was barely noticeable.

Claire smiled nervously. 'An accident.' She didn't bother to elaborate. 'So I am afraid I can't...' She gave a jerky gesture towards Desmona's outstretched hand; the hand fluttered a little then dropped.

Clearly picking up on the tension suddenly surrounding them all, Melanie let out another protesting cry. Desmona's eyes flicked from Claire to the baby, and in the sudden taut silence which followed something in her expression subtly altered.

'She is like you, Andreas,' she remarked casually enough, though.

'She is my daughter,' he answered just as casually. 'What else would you expect?'

No reply was forthcoming, but the silence lashed to and

fro with the kind of bitter words Claire could sense but not follow.

Then the silver eyes were shifting back to Claire, and the cold mask, which had slipped slightly, was suddenly back in place as Desmona politely excused herself before walking gracefully away along a formally set pathway that took her around the side of the house.

'Good grief,' Claire breathed as the air left her body in a single relieved whoosh. 'What was all that about?'

For a moment Andreas didn't answer, his attention thoughtfully fixed on Desmona's steadily receding figure. Then he surprised Claire with a short, sardonic laugh. 'You have just met the family choice for my bride,' he said dryly.

'Your late brother's *wife*?' she gasped, tipping her head back to stare at him in shocked disbelief.

He was already looking down at her, so their eyes clashed. The surface of her skin began to tingle, her insides along with it. She could feel herself beginning to fall into those devilish black eyes again and couldn't seem to do a single thing to stop it.

'Timo was a lot older than me,' Andreas was explaining, seemingly unaware of the strange sensations Claire was beginning to experience every single time she looked into those eyes now. 'They think I owe his widow something for inheriting on his death.'

'But that's archaic,' she denounced, having to struggle to keep her mind locked on the conversation and not on the man she was having the conversation with. 'When did your brother die?'

The bleak, pained look that came into his eyes occasionally was beginning to make more sense now, she realised as she watched it appear again. 'Just over a year ago,' he replied.

So, he had lost a wife he loved six years before, and a brother only recently. 'I'm sorry,' Claire murmured.

'So am I.' He smiled that brief grim smile. 'I miss him.'

'I know.' She nodded in understanding. 'You catch yourself looking round to speak to them only to feel that dreadful clutch of emptiness when you find they're not there and you remember...'

His dark lashes gave a flicker. Claire's breath caught on a softly inhaled little gasp when she saw the usual knock-back on its way. So she was totally unprepared for it when instead he bent his head and kissed her fully on her mouth.

If this was another punishing kiss for encroaching where he didn't want her to, then it didn't quite work out like that. Caught so off guard with her lips parted and her body relaxed, she was powerless to stop what happened next as she fell headlong into that kiss.

I don't need to be looking into those eyes to feel like this, she realised as her whole mouth softened and drew him deeper, touching tongues—tongues that caused a sharp, hot electric charge to go racing through her blood. It was devastating, the most passionate encounter she had ever experienced. And if he wasn't feeling it with her, then he was certainly feeling something that made a muffled groan break in his throat and his chest heave against her resting head before he completely caved in and threw himself passionately into that kiss.

If he hadn't been holding Melanie, Claire had a horrible feeling he would have fallen on her like a ravenous wolf. As it was his stance shifted slightly and the hand resting at her waist became a clamp to wedge her back hard up against the full length of his side with a need to increase and compound upon what was suddenly running rife between them.

It was crazy—totally crazy, she kept on telling herself over and over. This wasn't supposed to happen. This was a business arrangement. No intimacy.

No intimacy. But if this wasn't being intimate then she didn't know what was. And she could smell the clean spicy smell of him—was being enveloped by it—stormed by it! Even her bruised ribs weren't bothering to put up any protest at being clamped so tightly against him—they were too busy being under attack from the other side where her heart was pounding wildly in response to the whole mad, hot onslaught.

Then he groaned again, and in the next moment she was abruptly set free. In a dizzy haze of complete and utter disorientation, she reeled away. Legs like lead, eyes in a fog, she stumbled from beneath the terrace overhang and out into the sunshine.

'Where are you going?' His voice sounded hoarse and husky. But it brought her to a stop.

'I—don't know,' she answered honestly, too confused to care how stupid she must sound.

Or stupefied, she then thought numbly, and wished the grass beneath her feet would open up and swallow her whole so she didn't have to make herself turn around and face him.

Not that she needed to look to know exactly what she would see—a dark devil who had the kiss of hell in his repertoire, she thought fancifully.

A dark devil no less, who was cradling a sweet little baby on his arm, she added, and let out a strangled laugh that seemed to echo plaintively in the somnolent warmth of the afternoon quietness.

Yet he didn't sound like a devil when he said, 'Come back, Claire,' very gently. 'You're quite safe here; please believe me…'

Safe, she repeated to herself. Tears sprang. Wretchedly she blinked them away. Then, on a small, tight, thickened suck of air, she attempted to pull herself together before turning round again.

She didn't look at him—refused to do so as she made her shaking limbs carry her back into the shade. Coming to her side, he paused for a moment, and her senses began to sting in an agony of need for him to say not another word!

He must have sensed it and held his silence, which was something else she was realising about him—he picked up her feelings very easily.

Which made her what? Claire wondered dizzily as they

both began walking in silence along the terrace towards the door. Pathetically transparent? 'I...' Desperately she searched her foggy brain for something casual to say so she could pretend the kiss just hadn't happened. And found it when the sound of a car engine powering into life reminded her of Desmona. 'Does Desmona live here in this house?'

'She has her own apartment in Athens,' he replied. 'But she comes to visit my grandmother quite regularly. Claire, listen to me,' he then urged huskily.

'Oh, good,' she cut in, agitatedly aware he was going to say something about that wretched kiss, and equally sure she did not want to hear it. 'Then I won't have to watch my back for flying knives,' she joked, and managed to gain some reassurance from the fact that she *could* joke while she was feeling like this.

They turned together into a vast hallway with a white ceramic floor, cream walls and a white-painted staircase that swept gracefully upwards to a galleried landing above. It was all very grand. Very—

At which point her brain ground to a stop when she found herself confronted by a long line of shyly smiling and expectant faces.

Oh, what now? she groaned inwardly, eyeing the long row of what could only be the staff needed to run this big house, looking at the uniform neat pale pink dresses and white aprons the females were wearing, while it was white shirts and dark trousers for the men.

Then, on a sudden flashback to a few minutes ago, her face suffused with mortified colour. 'Do you think they saw us outside?' she breathed for his ears alone, while having a sudden horrendous vision of them all crowding at the windows to watch Andreas kissing her.

'If they did,' he drawled, 'then we will have no need to labour the game-plan.'

It hit her then just what had been going on outside. That kiss had been part of this deception! No impulse, she realised.

But merely part of his precious game-plan to make their liaison appear genuine.

She felt oddly cheated. No, worse than that. She felt used.

'Shall we get this over with?' he suggested, while she was still struggling with the appalling proof of just how ruthless this man could be!

With a light touch to the rigid line of her spine he prompted her into motion. For the next five minutes, face after face went by in a blur of smiles and curiously craning necks as his staff tried to get a peep at the sleeping baby lying in the crook of their employer's arm.

In fact the only face that registered was that of a young girl on the end of the row who reminded her of Althea. She stepped forward and shyly offered to take Melanie from Andreas. While Claire stood by, intensely conscious of everyone's eyes on her, Andreas exchanged a few words in Greek with the young girl before he handed over Melanie.

'I don't believe you put me through that,' she hissed when eventually he began leading the way up the staircase to the landing above, giving the staff the chance to crowd around the young girl holding Melanie.

'It was not set up for your benefit but for theirs,' he came back crushingly. 'They need to know who it is they are going to be dealing with since you will in effect be the lady of the house.'

Lady of the house? Claire almost tripped over the next stair in trembling dismay! His hand came out to steady her—she didn't even notice! 'But I can't order those people around, Andreas!' she protested, not noticing either that she had used his name for the first time in her urgency to get her point across. 'I just wouldn't know how!'

'You will get used to it,' he murmured indifferently.

'But I don't *want* to get used to it!' she snapped, and at last realised he was touching her again and angrily tugged her arm free.

'Fine,' he concurred, letting her go—but only, she suspected, because they had reached the top of the stairs anyway, so she wasn't likely to trip over again. 'Then let Lefka do it when she arrives,' he suggested carelessly.

She had forgotten all about Lefka, who, she had learned in London, presided over whichever household Andreas was staying in. So—yes, she thought in relief, let Lefka do it. And felt her pounding heart settle down to a steadier pace. She was used to dealing with Lefka...

She followed Andreas along a galleried upper landing to a glossy white-painted door that led, she discovered, to a suite of rooms very similar to the suite she had been allocated in his London home, only this suite was decorated in neutral shades of the palest gardenia and grey.

While Claire walked over to the window to check out the view, Andreas walked across the thick carpet to another door and pushed it open.

'My rooms,' he announced, bringing her swinging abruptly to face him. 'But no key,' he dryly pointed out. 'So you will just have to trust me to behave myself.'

Was he really insensitive enough to joke about it after *that* kiss? Claire wondered furiously, and turned her back on him to walk over to the other side of the room where she opened another door, hoping to find a bedroom where Melanie would sleep. But a bathroom done in colours to match the bedroom gleamed cleanly back at her.

'Where is Melanie going to sleep?' she turned to ask.

'In the nursery on the other side of the house,' he said. 'I will show you later...'

He was already striding towards the only other door left in the room to open. Claire watched him, wondering what could be left to uncover. She remembered the huge dressing room in the London house and once again was ruefully envisaging her sad wardrobe inside it.

The door came open at his touch, and he turned to Claire. 'Come and look,' he invited.

Not a dressing room, then, she assumed, walking curiously

forward—only to go still in a state of breathless surprise when she realised that she was not only right and that this was indeed a dressing room, but also that her wardrobe of clothes certainly would be lost inside it—amongst the racks and rails and shelves already filled to bursting with the most exquisite things she had ever seen.

Expensive clothes. Designer clothes. Some of them very formal evening clothes. Yet still the kind of modern clothes any fashion-conscious twenty-one-year-old would die to possess.

'For me?' she asked breathlessly.

'Yes,' he replied, and watched grimly the way her fingers trembled as she lifted them to cover equally tremulous lips.

'I don't know what to say,' she whispered.

'Your response says it for you,' he responded quietly.

'I will never be able to wear this much!' she cried, her eyes beginning to shine with unshed tears of excitement as those same trembling fingers reached out to touch a fine georgette top in smoky mauve with a matching shantung silk skirt to go with it.

'Try,' he invited.

Then she suddenly thought just what she was doing. 'You must think me very mercenary,' she groaned, turning to find him leaning lazily against the open door, his dark eyes fixed on her expressive face.

'I think you are exquisite,' he answered deeply, reaching out to touch his cool fingertips to the satin-smooth heat in one of her cheeks, his expression so unimaginably sombre that it trapped the air inside her chest.

Then he was turning away from her in that now familiarly abrupt way of his. 'Enjoy,' he invited with a careless wave of his hand. 'Enjoy.'

And he was gone, disappearing through the connecting door to his own room, leaving Claire standing there with her own palm now pressed where his fingertips had been. Her thoughts locked on that terrible—terrible expression she had glimpsed on his face before he'd walked away from her.

It hurt so much to see it that she had a sudden urge to run after him, throw her arms around his neck and tell him not to be so sad, for she loved him; surely that had to count for something—?

Is that what I'm doing? Claire asked herself starkly. Am I falling in love with him?

He picks you up off the road, dusts you off, takes you home and feeds you. He then sweeps all your troubles away by replacing them with a whole new set of troubles—and you decide he's the man to fall in love with?

Sold, she grimly mocked herself. For the price of a big house and a load of designer clothes, to the ruthlessly calculating man in the corner with the attitude problem worth falling in love with!

Well... Her chin came up, the light of a battle entering her eyes, though she knew the battle was now with herself. Marching forward, she firmly knocked on his door then swung it open.

'I want to talk to my aunt Laura,' she announced forcefully.

And thereby learned just how *he* must have felt when she'd walked out of the bathroom in his London home, with her robe hanging open down her naked front!

OK, she allowed as her senses roared into an overdrive she had never, ever before had to contend with. So he wasn't quite naked. But there was only one piece of clothing left on his big, sleek, muscle-rippling dark golden body for him to take off—and those black silk briefs were not hiding very much!

Certainly not the powerful build of his legs or the kind of muscular torso Atlas himself would envy! Wonderful wide shoulders, she listed bemusedly. Lean, powerful hips, and the dynamic evidence of a—

'Get the hell out of here!' he snarled.

Claire almost left her skin behind as she jumped in response. Her eyes flickered then focused too late—much too late—to save her own dignity, never mind his. For it was only then that she realised just where she had been staring!

She whipped out of that room as fast as her shaking legs could take her. Pulling the door shut behind her, she wilted weakly against the wall beside it, squeezing her eyes tight shut so she could beg whoever it was who could make these things happen that they take back the last thirty dreadful seconds!

No chance. She wasn't even allowed a few minutes to recover her composure before that damn door was shooting open again.

Pausing to scan the room for her, Andreas found her standing there cringing like an idiot against the wall with her eyes squeezed tightly shut. Swinging himself around, he slapped his hands on the wall at either side of her head so he could push his face up close to hers like the dark avenger in search of a victim.

'What the hell did you think you were doing barging into my room like that?' he raked at her furiously.

'I'm sorry,' she choked, feeling his angry breath warm on her face, but keeping her eyes shut because she still wasn't ready to take on board how she had been so crass as to stare at his body like that. 'I didn't think. I just—'

'Didn't think?' he interrupted. 'Have you any idea how close you came to completely embarrassing both of us?'

Oh, yes, she thought, with a telling little shudder, she had a very vivid idea how close she had come. 'I'm sorry,' she repeated. 'I'm sorry—I'm sorry!'

Small white teeth appeared, biting hard into her bottom lip, her only good hand clenching into a fierce fist while she tried very hard to dismiss the image that was still cruelly filling her head.

Another sigh rasped her face. 'You idiot,' he murmured, and the anger seemed to be easing out of him. 'Next time knock and wait until you are invited before opening that door, and save both our blushes.'

'Ditto,' she found the presence of mind to counter.

It took him a moment, then he huffed out a laugh. 'I suppose you do have a point,' he conceded. 'Are you all right?' he asked then. 'You have gone a really strange shade of puce. Never actually seen a man naked before, hmm?'

He was taunting her! she realised. 'Don't you dare laugh at me!' she flashed, her eyes shooting open in sheer reaction.

Oh, good grief. He was very close. She hadn't realised just how close until she found herself staring into those devilish black eyes bare inches away. But at least he'd stopped long enough to pull on a robe, she noted with relief.

'And of course I've seen men naked before,' she lied, lifting her chin to throw the words at him like a challenge. 'Loads of them as a matter of fact,' she added for good measure. 'And you weren't naked.'

'Oh, I don't know,' he drawled. 'I certainly felt it.'

His mocking tone sent her eyes tight shut again. This isn't really happening, she told herself firmly. It's all just a very bad dream.

This time it was a soft huff of laughter that brushed across her heated face. Then—thankfully—he straightened away from her. 'Now, what did you want?'

Claire shook her head. 'It doesn't matter.' In truth, she couldn't remember now what had sent her into his room like that.

'You mentioned your aunt, I seem to remember.' The rotten swine knew she had forgotten.

'Where is she?' she demanded. 'Why hasn't she been in touch with me?'

'Probably because it is more than her job is worth to try,' he answered laconically.

Claire frowned, beginning to relax a little now he had put a bit more distance between them. 'If you dislike her so much—' and it was obvious that he did '—then why do you employ her?'

His lips compressed, his dark eyes hooding over in a way that told Claire he wasn't going to answer that question even before he confirmed it. 'If you never take anything else from me, Claire, then take this small piece of advice,' he suggested very seriously. 'Forget your aunt. Or even that she works for me. She is not worthy of a single one of your thoughts. Now,' he added, giving her no chance to challenge all of that before he was turning back to his room, 'I am going for my shower. You have approximately half an hour to prepare yourself for an audience with my grandmother, by the way,' he told her blithely before shutting himself away.

His grandmother...? Couldn't he have told her that before?

'Oh, heck!' she gasped, and dropped everything else right out of her mind to make room for this much more nerve-racking prospect.

CHAPTER SIX

BOTH nervous and anxious about the coming ordeal, Claire rummaged quickly through the rails of her brand-new wardrobe of clothes, and eventually decided on a misty grey silk-lined linen dress that she felt she could easily slip into. Taking it through to the bedroom, she laid it on the bed.

But it was only while she was tackling the difficult task of pulling on a pair of fine silk hold-up stockings with only one hand to do it with that she suddenly realised there was no way she was going to be able to pull up the zip running the full length of the back of her chosen dress!

Puffing and panting from her excursions, she was standing there in her bra and panties feeling very hot and very flustered, and about to go and select something less difficult to put on, when a light knock sounded on the outer door.

Peering warily around a thin crack in the door, she was so relieved that it wasn't Andreas catching her in a state of undress yet again that she almost dragged the young maid into her room in her eagerness.

'Oh, thank goodness,' she sighed, smiling with relief. 'Do you speak English?' she asked hopefully, and at the girl's nod said, 'Then will you please help me to do up the zip on the back of this dress?'

Scurrying over to the bed, she snatched up the dress, feeling the seconds ticking ever further onwards towards her next ordeal when what she really wanted to do was lie down and rest because her neck was aching after having to take the weight of her wrist in its sling all day.

Never mind all the stress and tension, she tagged on hectically as she shimmied into the dress. 'What's your name?' she enquired curiously as the zip rasped up her backbone.

'My name is Lissa,' the maid replied shyly, probably wondering if Claire had any brains at all, when it had only been an hour ago that she had been introduced to her downstairs.

Which, Claire decided, was probably true because her brains seemed to have gone begging from the moment Andreas had dared to kiss her outside in the garden.

And remembering that right now was stupid! she scolded herself as her insides went haywire at the memory. Then she remembered the most recent scene that thoroughly outranked the one with the kiss. And the two together played merry havoc with just about every sensitive nerve she had in her system.

Oh, stop it! You don't have time to fall apart at the seams right now! she told herself crossly. She was just slipping her feet into a new pair of grey low-heeled shoes whilst carefully feeding her plastered wrist back into its support when another knock sounded.

At the connecting door.

Both Claire and the maid turned to stare at it, and, as quick as that, the tension was back, singing across the room to ricochet off that closed door and back at her—and that was without so much as setting eyes on the perpetrator of it all!

At least he's practising what he preaches, she noted wryly when the door remained resolutely shut. She moved to answer it—the little maid scurried in the opposite direction with a mumbled excuse.

Deserting the sinking ship, Claire thought. Then she was gritting her teeth and setting her chin before reaching for the door handle.

It was like opening the door on a hot oven. The power of this man's newly recognised sexuality flooded over her in burning waves. Stifled by it, she could neither breathe nor think. So she just stood there staring at him while his dark eyes hooded over as they began a slow scan of her from shining head to neatly shod feet.

Then she began to notice that he was wearing the most

casual clothes she had seen him in to date. The lightweight
chinos hung loosely from his narrow waistline; the white soft
cotton knit polo shirt moulded his well remembered torso like
a second skin.

No, don't think of that! she told herself sternly. 'Will I
do?' she asked, anxiously searching those unrevealing eyes
as they made the same journey back up her again.

To her consternation, he emitted a rather odd laugh. And
his head gave a small shake as if he couldn't believe what
he was actually seeing. Then those wretched dark eyes
flicked downwards again, prompting Claire's gaze to follow
them to discover what it was that was bothering him.

And at last she became aware of the incredible amount of
leg the short dress had left on show! Her mind shot off,
seeing through this man's eyes what his ninety-two-year-old
grandmother was going to see: a tall, leggy female who must
be a brazen hussy to wear a skirt this short! 'I'll get changed,'
she announced, turning jerkily away from him.

'You will not.' His hand capturing her good one stopped
her in her tracks. 'You will *do* fine,' he added softly at her
frowning expression.

'That wasn't what you were thinking when you first saw
me,' she pointed out candidly.

To her surprise, yet again he uttered one of those odd
laughs. 'You don't want to know what I was thinking,' he
mocked her dryly. Then, before she could respond to that, he
said, 'Come on, let's go.'

His hand tightened on her hand to keep her firmly beside
him when she would have pulled slightly away. And like that
they walked across her room and out onto the galleried landing. In silence she let him lead her, his hand warm around
hers and faintly comforting, which confused her rather because she knew she should be shying right away from his
touch.

At the head of the stairs he walked them beneath a deep
archway that led into another wing of the house. With no

natural light flooding in from the gallery, in here it was darker, and there was a different atmosphere—a hushed silence that felt slightly suffocating as they travelled along a carpeted corridor towards a pair of double doors at the other end.

'Where's Melanie?' Claire asked in a hushed whisper—it was most definitely a whispering kind of place.

'The nursery quarters are in the other wing,' Andreas informed her. 'She will not be meeting my grandmother today.'

'But I thought that she was the sole reason why we are both here at all.' She frowned in confusion.

'My grandmother is ninety-two.' He seemed to feel he needed to remind her. 'She lives by a different set of social morals than you or I do. She will not acknowledge Melanie until we are married.'

Oh, great, Claire thought heavily. I am about to meet a ninety-two-year-old puritan with the kind of moral codes that will file me under the heading marked 'loose woman' for being so free and irresponsible with my sexual favours!

The short dress was as big a mistake as she'd suspected it would be, she realised as she stood there with Andreas beside her, his arm casually resting across her narrow shoulders now while his grandmother inspected Claire.

Ninety-two was certainly old, Claire noted as she, in turn, studied the elderly lady. She looked thin and very frail, sitting there in an old-fashioned wing-backed chair which suited the old-fashioned possessions that surrounded her.

The light in the room was unnaturally dim, made so by a tall folding screen that had been pulled across the window, and the air was so warm it was stifling, yet his grandmother was draped from shoulders to feet in shawls and blankets as if the blood in her veins must be too slow to help keep her warm any more.

But the pair of beady amber eyes in her withered face were certainly very much alert. She snapped something at her grandson in Greek. He replied smoothly.

'You ought to be ashamed of yourself!' the old woman scolded, switching to scathing English.

'Resigned to my lot is the truth of it,' Andreas threw back lazily. 'The too old and the too young.' He dryly marked the distinction. 'Both of them the bane of my wretched life.'

To Claire's surprise the old woman laughed, the sound shrilling the stifling air with a high-pitched cackle. 'I will speak to you later,' she informed her grandson once she had recovered her composure.

Then she flicked her sharp eyes back onto Claire's face. Claire stiffened in response, readying herself for the blast of criticism she sensed was coming her own way next. The hand Andreas had curved around her shoulder gave a gentle squeeze as if in reassurance. He was still very relaxed himself—which had to mean something, Claire told herself as she waited.

As perceptive as her grandson at picking up other people's vibrations, the old lady challenged, 'Scared of me, are you? Wondering what I am going to say to you as you stand there next to my grandson with your short skirt and your long legs enough to tempt a saint out of celibacy. Did your mother never warn you that men are weak of the flesh?'

'My mother is dead,' Claire answered levelly.

'Your father, then.' Death, it seemed, held no excuse to the old woman.

'Dead also.' It was Andreas who answered this time, his tone revealing just the slightest hint of a warning. 'And treading carelessly on other people's feelings is unacceptable, even for a dying old woman.'

Claire's shocked gasp was ignored as the old woman flicked her eyes back to Andreas and glowered at him. 'Oh, come over here,' she then commanded him impatiently. 'I want my kiss now...'

At last he deserted his post beside Claire, walking gracefully across the room to bend over the old lady. They embraced, exchanged a few softly spoken Greek words that somehow made Claire feel rather sad.

'You next!' the sharp voice then snapped out at Claire as Andreas straightened again.

Going over to her, Claire obediently bent to brush a kiss on the old woman's lined cheek. 'What did you do to your hand?' she then asked curiously.

Claire explained. The old woman grimaced then pushed back the blanket to reveal her left arm, which she tried to move but clearly couldn't. 'Snap,' she murmured ruefully.

A joke, Claire realised, even if it was a wretched joke. And impulsively she bent to drop another sympathetic kiss upon a withered cheek. The old lady didn't reject it, and there was something very close to a sad vulnerability in her eyes as Claire straightened again.

But the voice was as surly as ever when she said, 'Now go away, the pair of you; I'm tired. I will see you later, Andreas, before I retire,' she prompted as Claire moved back to his side.

'Of course,' he nodded, making Claire aware that this must be something he always did when he was here.

'But you come back tomorrow to discuss your wedding dress,' Claire was then commanded. 'And we will see if we cannot add ten years to your age to save this family from another scandal.'

Another—? Claire thought sharply. But that was as far as that thought went as Andreas placed his hand on the base of her spine and urged her into movement.

'I like her exactly as she is,' he threw over his shoulder in a firm warning.

'You think we do not already know that?' the old woman snarled scathingly after him.

He just laughed and was still laughing when the door closed behind them. 'It keeps her will alive to spar with me.' He seemed constrained to explain the banter between the two of them.

'Yes, I realise that,' Claire nodded as they began walking back down the corridor.

He nodded too, pacing beside her. 'I know she is surly,' he added after a moment. 'But she feels the weight of her own helplessness. It makes her—'

'Surly,' Claire acknowledged. 'At least while she snaps people listen.'

'Yes.' He sounded almost relieved she understood that. 'But she means no harm by it. And, as she will no doubt tell you herself, she does not have the time or the energy to find out what she wants to know by more devious methods. So she jumps straight in there. She meant no offence regarding your mother and father.'

'None was taken.' Claire frowned, wondering, as they walked along, why he felt it necessary to explain all of this to her. 'Actually,' she added, 'I liked her.'

'Good,' he murmured as they reached the arch that would take them back into the other part of the house.

Claire stepped sideways slightly so they could both move through it. Andreas did the same—and the front of their bodies brushed. Claire stopped breathing. She had a horrible feeling that he had done the same. Tension was rife. She attempted to break it by sliding away from him—but, on a thickened sigh that was all the warning she got, Andreas placed the flat of his palm on the centre of her back, drew her harder against him—and took hungry possession of her mouth.

It was no use trying to delude herself that this kiss was anything other than it was because it didn't pretend to be. It was need, pure and simple. Even Claire, with her inexperience of these things, recognised that telling little fact as she was pressed back into a darkened corner of the arch and held there by the kind of need that was not going to take no for an answer.

Not that she was saying no—or considering saying it. Because from the moment his mouth moulded to the shape of her mouth her lips parted to welcome him. With his expertise to show her the way, she delved into the kind of heated passion that was utterly new to her. She felt hot and breathless, the dim quietness of the hallway helping to fill her head with a steamy mist that made him and what he was doing to her the only thing that mattered.

His hand drifted downwards to splay at the base of her spine so he could gently urge her into deeper contact with that part of him that so clearly needed it. He was aroused and pulsing; her gasp of awareness was breathed into his mouth. His other hand was making long stroking movements down her body, stimulating senses she hadn't even known were there but made her subside against him in drowning pleasure.

It went on and on, growing deeper and more intimate with each heated second as his hand made its way down to one of her silk-covered thighs then began a pleasurable stroking upwards again. Long fingers made contact with bare flesh above her lace edged stocking. Claire responded by arching her spine closer to him.

In all her life she had never experienced anything like it. It was hungry, it was intense, and it was deeply, deeply sensual, the whole thing coiling around them in burning tendrils of pleasure that poured fire into her veins.

A door opened somewhere down the quiet corridor. They broke apart like guilty teenagers.

Both dazed and momentarily dysfunctional, he muttered something—a curse, Claire suspected. Then another—and another while he blocked her from sight with his big body as someone walked down the hallway and in through another door.

By then she had wilted weakly into the corner, eyes closed, heart fighting to regain control of itself.

He seems to like pinning me up against walls, she found herself thinking, and choked on a laugh that wasn't really a laugh. She couldn't believe she could be thinking such ridiculously flippant things at a time like this!

'Don't,' he rasped softly, and his fingers threaded themselves into her hair so his thumb pad could stroke gently across the new pulsing fullness he had brought to her mouth.

Don't—what? Claire asked herself half hysterically. Don't laugh? Don't cry? Don't fall apart at the seams in confusion because what just happened was not supposed to happen?

'Don't look to yourself to find the culprit... '

He thought she was blaming herself? Claire glared at the floor between their two pairs of feet and mulishly refused to answer.

After a few taut seconds of this stubborn refusal to offer him a single word, he sighed heavily and his hand fell away, leaving her traitorous mouth pulsing all the hotter. 'It is my fault, not yours. I am—attracted to you,' he confessed, seemingly forced into saying that by her silence. 'But you can trust me not to let this—situation get out of control...'

Could she? At last she found the strength to straighten away from the wall. There had been no control in either of them only a few moments ago. And it was getting worse every time they kissed like that!

'I do not seduce innocent virgins,' was his final stiff offering of what she presumed was supposed to be reassurance.

Where it came from she did not know, because she had never done anything like it before. But, like a cobra rearing up for a sudden attack, she came away from that wall and pushed him violently out of her way, then stalked angrily off, shaking and trembling and wishing the pompous devil in hell!

It was the word 'innocent' that had triggered her reaction; she knew that because the condescending sound of his voice saying it was still buzzing inside her head!

Because the last thing she felt right now was *innocent!* She thought crossly as she paced the pale grey carpet in her room. What she did feel was hot and restless and excited!

If it hadn't been for Lissa, the little maid, coming to offer to show her where the nursery was, she probably would have started throwing things just to ease her wretched frustration!

I hate him, she thought as she went off to spend the next couple of hours helping where she could with Melanie.

I hate him! she repeated after spending ages arming herself ready to face him across the dinner table, only to find that the lucky devil had escaped to calmer places. 'A business dinner,' the staff called it.

Claire begged to differ. She already recognised the tactics. Playing the advance and retreat game was just another fetish of his. So, having advanced, he was now in retreat, hiding, because he was afraid she might decide to call the whole thing off if he stayed around to let her!

The next morning she came awake to find Althea standing over her with a breakfast tray carrying her usual tea and toast. Surprised, she pulled herself up the pillows then blinked the sleep from her eyes. 'Hello. When did you arrive?' she asked curiously.

'Late last night.' Althea smiled. 'Andreas wanted to leave you to sleep this morning,' she then explained apologetically. 'But his grandmother is already asking for you. So...'

Enough said, Claire acknowledged ruefully as she watched Althea place the tray across her lap and begin pouring her tea for her, just the way she liked it.

After that, the two of them fell back into a harmonious routine they had perfected during her stay at the London house. Half an hour later, showered, dressed in a pair of tailored pale blue trousers and a simple white top, she was walking along the gallery to attend the royal summons.

Althea was with her, by order of the grandmother, so Claire had been told. Knocking lightly on the old lady's door, they then waited for the terse, 'Enter!' before stepping inside.

The room looked quite different this morning. The tall screen had been moved from the window to allow the morn-

PLAY
RUN
FOR THE
ROSES

and get
THREE FREE GIFTS!

HOW TO PLAY:

1. With a coin, carefully scratch off the silver box at the right. Then check the claim chart to see what we have for you — **2 FREE BOOKS** and a **FREE GIFT**—**ALL YOURS FREE!**

2. Send back the card and you'll receive two brand-new Harlequin Presents® novels. These books have a cover price of $3.99 each in the U.S. and $4.50 each in Canada, but they are yours to keep absolutely free.

3. There's no catch. You're under no obligation to buy anything. We charge nothing — ZERO — for your first shipment. And you don't have to make any minimum number of purchases — not even one!

4. The fact is, thousands of readers enjoy receiving books by mail from the Harlequin Reader Service®. They enjoy the convenience of home delivery...they like getting the best new novels at discount prices, BEFORE they're available in stores... and they love their *Heart to Heart* subscriber newsletter featuring author news, horoscopes, recipes, book reviews and much more!

5. We hope that after receiving your free books you'll want to remain a subscriber. But the choice is yours — to continue or cancel, any time at all! So why not take us up on our invitation, with no risk of any kind. You'll be glad you did!

Visit us online at
www.eHarlequin.com

This surprise mystery gift
Could be yours **FREE** –
When you play
RUN for the ROSES

Scratch
Here
See Claim Chart

YES! I have scratched off the silver box. Please send me the 2 FREE books and gift for which I qualify! I understand that I am under no obligation to purchase any books, as explained on the back and opposite page.

RUN for the ROSES	Claim Chart
♛ ♛ ♛	2 FREE BOOKS AND A MYSTERY GIFT!
♛ ♛	1 FREE BOOK!
♛	TRY AGAIN!

NAME   (PLEASE PRINT CLEARLY)

ADDRESS

APT.#   CITY

STATE/PROV.   ZIP/POSTAL CODE

306 HDL C25M

106 HDL C25D
(H-P-OS-05/00)

Offer limited to one per household and not valid to current
Harlequin Presents® subscribers. All orders subject to approval.

The Harlequin Reader Service® — Here's how it works:

Accepting your 2 free books and gift places you under no obligation to buy anything. You may keep the books and gift and return the shipping statement marked "cancel." If you do not cancel, about a month later we'll send you 6 additional novels and bill you just $3.34 each in the U.S., or $3.74 each in Canada, plus 25¢ delivery per book and applicable taxes if any.* That's the complete price and — compared to cover prices of $3.99 each in the U.S. and $4.50 each in Canada — it's quite a bargain! You may cancel at any time, but if you choose to continue, every month we'll send you 6 more books, which you may either purchase at the discount price or return to us and cancel your subscription.

*Terms and prices subject to change without notice. Sales tax applicable in N.Y. Canadian residents will be charged applicable provincial taxes and GST.

ing sun to stream in, and was now shielding a corner of the room.

And what had looked like heavy and dark old-fashioned bits and bobs yesterday suddenly looked interestingly aged, making Claire want to walk around the room and study them.

But the old lady was sitting there in her chair by the window looking cross and impatient. 'What time do you call this?' she snapped. 'We get up at dawn in this country, not the end of the day.'

Knowing it was only nine o'clock in the morning, Claire smiled at this gross piece of exaggeration. 'But at least I came here first and without even going to see my baby,' she remarked, taking her lead from the way Andreas had spoken to his grandmother yesterday, and deciding to take her on when she snapped.

'What baby?' the old woman shot back.

'The...' Ah, Claire thought, biting back the sarcastic reply she had been about to make. Taboo subject, she recalled as those beady eyes dared her—just dared her to say anything more about Melanie.

The frail old head nodded when Claire remained wryly silent. Then she was turning her attention on Althea. 'Althea, go into my bedroom and bring the dress that is hanging on my wardrobe,' she commanded.

With an obedient nod, Althea hurried away, and Claire was ordered to come and sit down in the chair set beside the old woman.

'Now,' Andreas's grandmother said once Claire was seated, 'you will explain to me, please, while Althea is away, what you have done to upset my grandson. He was here an hour or two ago,' she informed Claire, 'and he was bad-tempered and restless. Have you two argued?'

No, Claire thought ruefully, we just kissed each other senseless. Then I pushed him away and he went off in a huff! 'I haven't even seen him since I left here with him yesterday.' She avoided the straight answer.

'You mentioned his first wife to him; that is what you did,' the old woman decided.

Claire immediately stiffened. 'I did not,' she denied.

Those amber eyes that had so much life left in them while the body they belonged to was wasting away fixed on her narrowly, looking at her as if they had the ability to see right through the blueness of her eyes to the brain that worked behind them.

'Then take my advice, young woman,' she said eventually. 'If you care anything for Andreas, then never mention her to him, do you hear?'

Yes, I hear, Claire thought, inwardly shocked by the amount of passion the old lady had fed into her words. But I don't understand.

And she was not offered enlightenment—except... 'He needs no more heartache dishing out to him—especially by a nubile young English girl with independent ways and legs that reach up to her armpits! Ah!' she then exclaimed in pleasure as Althea came back into the room. 'This is what I want to show you!'

And the other subject was dropped, leaving Claire sitting there wondering bleakly just how deeply Andreas had loved his first wife for even his grandmother to worry about the fragile state of his emotions.

But—nubile? she then repeated to herself with a grin. Such an old-fashioned word! Yet, coming as it had from this hypercritical old woman, she found it rather a compliment.

'Why the grin?' the sharp tongue demanded. 'You don't like my dress? You think it is funny?'

Dress—what dress? Claire frowned, clicking her eyes into focus on what Althea was carefully holding up so the long skirt didn't touch the ground.

'Oh!' she cried out as she jumped to her feet. 'How absolutely lovely!'

'You like it,' the old woman sighed in satisfaction—then

instantly went back to being stern. 'It was my wedding dress. Now it is yours.'

'Oh, but I can't—'

Even as Claire turned to gasp out her protest, the old lady was talking over her. 'Of course you can!' she snapped. 'It is my wish! So try it on—try it on and let us see how little different my young figure was to yours at your age!'

She sounded so animated—alive and excited—that Claire didn't have the heart to protest a second time. But as she looked back at the long, soft lines of the beautiful dress she felt like a dreadful fraud.

A deceiver of a vulnerable old woman.

But, by the time she emerged from behind the tall screen, having had Althea help her out of her clothes and into the dress, she was already head over heels in love with the dress.

Made of an intricately worked handmade lace worn over the finest silk under-dress, it skimmed her slender body as if it had been made for it. The neckline scooped gently over her breasts. The long fitted sleeves fastened by tiny pearl buttons that ran from wrist to elbow—one of which had to remain unfastened because of her cumbersome plaster-cast. The skirt was a little short, finishing just above her ankle, but even that didn't seem to matter.

It was the nineteen twenties at its most poetic. It was simply exquisite.

And just to see that sheen of tearful joy enter those tired eyes made wearing it a pleasure.

The old lady sighed, then ran on in hushed Greek that didn't need translating for Claire to understand that she was overwhelmed by what she was seeing.

Herself maybe? Claire pondered. Was this old woman who was so very close to the end of her life suddenly seeing herself when she was at the beginning?

'You will do—you will do,' the old lady murmured huskily. Then she said, with a return of her old sharpness, 'Nubile, eh? Was I not nubile also?' she declared triumphantly.

And Claire couldn't help laughing even though she was still feeling like a terrible fraud.

'You will wear it next week when you marry my grandson and he will bless the day he found you because that dress is lucky,' she promised, having no idea that Claire had switched off from the moment she'd mentioned marriage next week, which was news to her. 'I had fifty years of happiness with my husband before the cancer took him. You will have the same luck. You mark my word, child. That dress is lucky...'

'But this whole thing is getting out of control, Andreas!'

Claire was pleading with him across the width of his study desk, having come to search him out the moment she had been dismissed from his grandmother.

'She wants me to wear her own wedding dress!'

'You don't like it?' Sleek eyebrows arched in haughty enquiry.

'Like it?' Claire repeated incredulously. 'It's old, it's handmade, it's utterly unique and it's exquisite!' she sighed. 'But she *loves* that dress, Andreas!' she told him painfully. 'And she loves you! Yet here we are intending to dupe her any which way you want to look at it!'

The only response she got to that was the slow lowering of lazy lashes then the same slow lifting of them again. But then, he was the ice man today, Claire noted impatiently. Yesterday hadn't happened. He had clearly dismissed it from his mind.

'Do something!' she snapped in sheer frustration.

'What would you like me to do?' he asked quietly. 'Go and tell her that this is all nothing but a lie?'

'No,' she sighed, hating him for his smooth simplicity! 'I just feel—' She sighed again, and turned her back on him so she could slump wearily against the desk. 'I hate liars,' she said. 'Yet here I am, lying to everybody I speak to.'

'Is she happy?'

Claire dipped her head to stare at her shoes. 'Yes,' she said.

'Did the dress fit you as it must have fitted her more than seventy years ago?'

'Yes,' she said again, seeing the joy in that old woman's face when she'd seen herself as she would have looked all those years ago.

To her consternation he gave a soft laugh. 'She told me it would.' He explained the reason for the laugh. 'Last night, after having met you, she laid a wager with me that if the dress fitted you then I must buy it from her for you to wear on our wedding day. Oh, don't misunderstand,' he said quickly as Claire turned to stare at him. 'She is a shrewd old thing, and she loves a good wager. The dress is a museum piece and practically priceless. She knows this. She means to fleece me, and will enjoy doing so.'

And thereby keep the weak lifeblood flowing through her veins that little bit longer while they haggle, Claire concluded, beginning to see again what her guilty conscience had blinded her to—the fact that this man was willing to do anything to keep his grandmother alive.

Today it was a wedding dress. Tomorrow it would be something else. Then there was a wedding to plan and a great-grandchild to meet and...

Without really knowing she was doing it, she began planning and plotting herself. 'She wants the wedding to take place next week.' She frowned. 'Perhaps, if I insist that we put it off until my plaster-cast comes off, it will—'

But already Andreas was shaking his dark head, the expression on his suddenly grave face enough to tell her why.

'She hasn't got that long?' Claire questioned thickly.

He didn't answer with a straight yes or no. 'She knows what she is doing,' he murmured. 'Let her set her own timetable, hmm?'

A timetable... She shivered, hating the concept so much

that she sprang abruptly away from the desk. 'I'm going to see Melanie,' she told him as she walked quickly to the door.

For at least Melanie was everything that was bright and optimistic about life, whereas—

'Claire—one more moment of your time before you go, if you please,' that infuriatingly level voice requested.

It reminded her of a softly spoken headmaster she'd once had, who'd used to intimidate everyone with the simple use of the spoken word. Resenting the sensation, she spun around to glare at him. Seeing the glare, he responded with that brief grim smile she despised so much.

'At the risk of infuriating you even more,' he drawled, 'I have to warn you that there will be a party here tomorrow night. My family wish to meet you before the wedding takes place,' he explained, watching the varying changes in expression cross her face. Annoyance, trepidation then eventually dismay. 'It will take the form of a—betrothal celebration.' Smoothly he poured oil on the burning waters.

'No,' she refused, point-blank and unequivocally.

The leather chair he was sitting in creaked slightly as he sat back into it, the morning sunlight pouring in through the window behind him putting his features into shadow so she couldn't see whether he was smiling that smile.

But she knew it was still there! 'I've done everything you've asked me to do to make this lie work for you!' she informed him hotly. 'But I will not be paraded in front of your family to be scoffed at because they think I am a—a fallen woman who trapped you with a baby!'

Despite the sun behind him, she saw his eyes flash. 'Let only one of my family be so crass as to scoff at you and they will never be welcome in my home again.' At last he sounded as if he had some emotions left. 'But if that is your wish—' he stood up, and there was nothing calm or cold in the way that he did it '—then of course I will accede to it. I will go and inform my grandmother right now that she must shelve that particular plan.'

MICHELLE REID 103

His grandmother. He was agreeing to this party thing because his grandmother wanted it.

She was only agreeing to any of this for Melanie's sake. Grandmother—Melanie. Melanie—grandmother.

What about Claire? she wondered bitterly.

'Oh, have your stupid party,' she snapped. 'But don't blame me if they all think that you've lost your marbles when they see me!'

CHAPTER SEVEN

SHE was still angry about the emotional blackmail being used on her the next evening as she finished getting ready for the party.

So the dress was a defiance.

Claire knew that even as she stood in front of the mirror frowning in trepidation at the reflection that was coming back at her. Made of pale blue high-stretch gossamer-fine silk tulle, the flimsy bodice was supported by bootlace-slim halter-style straps that held the two triangles of fine fabric over her breasts. From there it followed the contours of her shape with such an unremitting faithfulness that it really was the most daringly thought-provoking garment.

She looked naked beneath it—felt naked! Though she knew that she wasn't if you took into account the tiniest pair of smooth silk briefs and a pair of white hold-up silk stockings. But nervous anxiety was making the hard tips of her nipples protrude to add to the illusion. And because the fabric clung so lovingly to her warm flesh she could even see the way the point high on her stomach between her ribcage was pulsing in tense anticipation of the evening to come.

'I can't wear this,' she muttered on a sudden arrival of common sense that should have hit a lot sooner.

Standing behind her, carefully teasing the final gold-silk strands of a natty fantail knot into which she was dressing her hair, Althea paused to glance over Claire's shoulder.

'I think you are so brave,' Althea confided—which helped not a tiny bit because she didn't feel brave at all!

Not any longer, anyway. This afternoon when she'd picked this dress out off the line of other evening dresses she had been feeling brave—brave, bold and brazen! she mocked herself deridingly. Seeing herself *boldly* taking on all those critical looks she just knew she was going to receive for not being their first choice of bride for their lord and master.

But now, with reality hovering over her like the shadow of a giant black-winged eagle preparing to swoop, her fickle emotions had flipped over into cowardice. And she knew now with absolute certainty that she just was not going to be able to carry this off!

A knock sounded lightly on the connecting door.

That pulse-point between her ribcage gave a large throb, and she froze. So did Althea, her gentle brown eyes fixing on Claire's pale face in the mirror. And silence rained down on top of both of them in a fine sprinkle of flesh-tingling static.

How much Althea and her parents actually knew for a fact about Claire's relationship with their employer Claire didn't really know. She thought that they at least suspected its lack of authenticity. After all, did Andreas look like the kind of man that seduced women like her?

But he does seduce me. She instantly contradicted that remark. Those increasingly passionate kisses are definitely seductive. And every time his dark hooded eyes settle on me now I feel dreadfully seduced even though he is trying his level best to pretend that it isn't happening.

'What do you want to do?' Althea whispered in a hushed little voice.

Die a thousand deaths by a thousand knives rather than open that door! she thought helplessly.

At least you've managed to put on some make-up. She allowed herself that one small consolation. Discovering today that she was now able to use the fingers on her right hand for light tasks meant that she had been able to do a lot more things for herself—one of them being the application of a light shadow to her eyelids, some mascara to her lashes without smearing it all over the place, and a rose-pink lipstick that gave her soft mouth a fullness that had not been there before.

She looked much better for that, even if she did say so herself.

You're not so bad-looking, you know, she informed that reflection. And despite its daring the dress is truly exquisite—the typically fashionable thing any woman slender enough to carry it off would wear today!

The knock sounded again, and she grimly pulled herself together. You've created your own monster here, Claire! she told that frightened face in the mirror. Now live with her!

With that little lecture to bolster her courage, Claire watched her chin come up, soft pink-painted mouth firming a little as the light of defiance sparked back into her eyes.

Seeing it happen, Althea took a step back in silent retreat. And when Claire turned away from the mirror to walk over to the connecting door Althea melted out of the room without another word spoken between them.

The way he was dressed, in a conventional black dinner suit, white dress shirt and black bow-tie, was the first thing Claire noticed as she pulled open the door. And the second thing was that he looked big and dark and dauntingly so-phisticated.

Her pulse quickened; she tried to steady it. He opened his mouth to say something light and ordinary—then stopped when his eyes actually focused on her properly.

Claire gave up trying to control her pulse when it broke free and just went utterly haywire as his gaze rippled over her. There was really no other way to describe it since that was exactly what her skin did as he inspected her slowly from the top of her shining head to rose-pink-painted toenails peeping out from the tips of her strappy silver shoes.

And he wasn't pleased by what he was seeing; she could see that immediately in the way his parted mouth snapped shut then tightened. 'Taking us all on, are you?' he drawled with super-dry sardonicism.

'I don't know what you're talking about,' she answered coldly.

He smiled that smile. 'Then let me put it this way,' he offered. 'I don't think there is going to be any doubt in the minds of anyone here tonight why I find myself having to marry you.'

'Lies can be such uncomfortable things sometimes, don't you think?' She acidly mocked all of that. 'But this one you will have to live with,' she then informed him. 'Because I am not going to cover myself up just to save your embarrassment.'

His sleek black brows shot up. 'Did I say I was embarrassed?'

You didn't have to, Claire thought, and turned away from him as an unexpected wave of disappointment hit. Even with defiance flying as high as a kite from her, she discovered, to her annoyance, that she had still been looking for his reassurance, not his disapproval.

Needing something to do to keep her muddled emotions hidden, she was glad that she had it—in the form of a white stretch-silk sleeve Althea had cleverly fashioned for her to wear over her plaster-cast.

It was waiting for her on her dressing table, and she walked over to get it, stingingly aware of those dark eyes taking in the amount of naked back the wretched dress left exposed.

'Where is your sling?' he enquired levelly after a few moments.

'I don't need it any more,' she said—then, with a half lift of one slender white shoulder, added, 'Well, not all the time anyway.'

'Here—allow me...'

A long-fingered hand appeared from behind her to take the white sleeve from her grasp. 'To cover your cast, I presume?' he said lightly.

The temptation to snatch it back from him and tell him

she could manage very well by herself almost—almost got the better of her. But even in the strange antagonistic mood she was in she knew that would be just too childish.

So she stood silent and still while he came to stand in front of her—her very own giant black-winged eagle, she mused as the feeling of being swooped down on overwhelmed her again. But then, she might be tall at five feet eight inches but he was one hell of a lot taller.

Taller, wider, bigger, darker, she listed as he picked up her injured wrist and began feeding the sleeve over the plaster-cast protecting it.

'Is the age thing a big problem to you, Claire?' he asked her quietly.

Older, tougher, calmer, cooler—the list went on. She gave a shake of her head in reply to his question.

'Perhaps you are still angry with me because I—over-stepped the boundaries of our arrangement, then.'

Wiser, she added. Because it hadn't really hit her until he'd said it out loud that this was exactly the reason why she was feeling as emotionally confused as she was.

'You blow hot and cold all the time,' she felt constrained to answer. 'I just don't know how to respond to that.'

'Then I apologise,' he murmured rather grimly.

Gracious, too, she added to the growing list. Because I'd have cut my own throat before I'd have had the grace to apologise as quickly and as sincerely as that.

Giving that small shrug with her shoulder again in ac-knowledgement of his apology, she then added a small sigh. 'It isn't going to be easy for me, you know, having to deal with all of these people who are coming here tonight, know-ing what they will all be thinking when they look at me.'

'I know.'

'Althea said she thought I was brave to dress myself up like this for the party. But I'm not brave, not really. I'm just...' She ran out of words on a discontented sigh.

'Trying to cope the best way you can.' He supplied them for her.

Silly tears tried to fill her eyes because now she was having to add understanding and gentle and sympathetic to her list and it really couldn't get any longer!

Yes, it can. She then had to amend that thought as he put his hand to her cheek and used his thumb to gently draw her chin up so he could look gravely into her swimming blue eyes. Because he was touching her for real rather than touching her through the protection of her plaster-cast, and she now had to add dangerous to that list because his touch made her feel so—!

He bent down to brush his mouth across hers, and the list was halted right then and there as it suddenly raced away from her in a mad, frantic blur of sizzling adjectives.

'Althea should have said beautiful and brave,' he murmured huskily as he drew away again.

So he did like the way she looked! If Claire could have seen her own eyes then, she knew it must have been like watching a dark shadow pass over and the sun coming out.

He smiled; so did she—the first real smile she had offered him in days. And while she continued to stand there feeling starry-eyed and breathless he picked up her other hand and slid something onto one of her fingers.

'A betrothal ring for my betrothed,' he murmured lightly as Claire glanced down then went perfectly still when she found herself staring at the most enchanting little diamond cluster ring she had ever set eyes on. 'It is a necessary part of the game-plan.'

The game-plan. Her heart thumped in her breast. How could she keep forgetting the game-plan?

'And it fits, too,' he added in that same lightly teasing vein. 'Which means Grandmother is going to make me pay for the pleasure of placing it here.'

'It's your grandmother's ring?' Swallowing her silly sense of let-down, Claire glanced up at him questioningly.

'The first of many my grandfather gave her,' he said with a small grimace. 'But this was her favourite. Do you like it?'

'It's a beautiful ring,' she murmured softly; it was not big enough to be ugly, not small enough to be cheap. 'Thank you for allowing me to wear it tonight,' she added, belatedly remembering her manners. 'I promise to take precious care of it for you.'

He had been about to move away from her when she said that. But now he stopped. 'It is yours to keep,' he stated rather curtly. 'I was not expecting to get it back.'

But Claire shook her head. 'No.' This ring did not belong to her and it never would. She could accept the new wardrobe of clothes and the luxury lifestyle she was being treated to here, because they only cost money and, as she had already learned with Andreas, money was a commodity he had more than enough of. But this ring—like the wedding dress—was different. Both had feelings attached to them, memories, for an old lady that belonged to this family, not to Claire, who was only passing through, so to speak.

He knew what she was thinking. She could feel him reading the sombre thoughts as they passed over her face. As she stood there with baited breath, waiting for him to start arguing the point with her, he surprised her by not doing that at all.

'You have integrity, Claire,' he murmured quietly. 'That is a rare commodity; try not to lose it.'

'Integrity?' she repeated, sending him a wry little smile that thoroughly mocked the suggestion. 'Where is the integrity in marrying someone you don't love, even if it benefits the both of us?' she asked him cynically.

He didn't answer, and she didn't blame him because there really was no answer that did not confirm she was telling the truth.

'Come on,' he prompted rather harshly instead. 'It is time for us to go and greet our guests.'

And that small amount of harmony they had managed to

create between them withered and died as they both remembered what this was really all about: a stranger's child that he, for no apparent reason, had decided to adopt as his own. For the first time since he had talked her into this, Claire began to question his reasoning because, knowing him better now than she had when they'd struck this deal, she could no longer accept that he needed to legally adopt Melanie to make this deception work.

After all, no one yet had questioned his claim that Melanie was his child. And if he genuinely needed an heir that badly, then why not find himself an olive-skinned boy-child? Unless choosing a girl was all part of the deception—a clouding of the scent to keep people's minds working on the wrong problem.

Could he be that devious? That tactically calculating? Glancing up at him as they began the long walk down the wide staircase, she saw the ruthlessness and cynicism etched into his dark profile and thought with a shiver, Yes, he can be that calculating.

Which still did not answer the question as to why he was determined to make it all legal. For if this was for his grandmother's sake, and from what he had already prepared Claire to expect his grandmother would not be around for very much longer, Melanie was too young to feel the loss of a father who was not her real father in the first place.

So what was really going on here? She frowned thoughtfully.

'Stop worrying,' he scolded levelly beside her. 'I won't let them eat you.'

But they did—or almost did—with curious looks laced with a disbelief that none of them seemed able to keep hidden, which made her feel uncomfortably like an alien being who was trying to infiltrate their selective society.

Though, to be fair, no one was openly rude or questioning. The older element said teasing things to Andreas in Greek to which he replied with smooth aplomb. The younger ones—

especially the men—ogled Claire in a way that made her blush and earned them a light but real warning to watch their manners from Andreas.

All very protective, very—possessive of him, she acknowledged. Like the way he kept her left hand enclosed in his right hand all the way through the ordeal while cheeks were brushed against cheeks in typical continental fashion.

'See, it was not so bad in the end, was it?' he drawled when the introductions were over.

Where were your eyes? she wanted to counter. But, 'No,' was what she actually said.

One person in particular gave her reason to feel really uncomfortable. Desmona glided in through the door looking absolutely stunning in the kind of dramatically simple black sheath gown that made Claire stingingly aware of her own complete lack of sophistication.

But she had to admire the way the other woman coped with the small silence that fell on her entrance.

The rejected one, that silence was shouting. Yet not by a flicker of her silver-grey eyes did she reveal any response to that.

She kissed Andreas on both cheeks and exchanged softly spoken words with him in Greek that had him smiling sardonically as he answered. Then she was turning to Claire, and for the next few minutes really impressed her as she smiled pleasantly and asked after Melanie.

As Desmona eventually moved away, it suddenly occurred to Claire that her being here to meet them on their arrival in Greece could have been pre-planned with this awkward moment in mind.

'A very classy lady, don't you think?' Andreas remarked.

'I feel sorry for her,' she confessed, watching the other woman join a group of people and begin talking lightly as if this were just any old social affair.

'Then don't,' was his rather curt rejoinder. 'For she is the sleeping panther in our midst whose teeth are none the less still sharp even though she is not baring them at present.'

As a clear warning to beware—though of what Claire wasn't sure—it certainly sent a cold shiver chasing down her spine.

She found that out later when Desmona decided to sink those teeth into Claire's shaky self-confidence.

Feeling flushed and breathless after having been danced around the large hallway by a rather enthusiastic old gentleman called Grigoris who was apparently to give her away at her wedding, Claire stood on the sidelines, alone for the first time since the whole extravaganza had begun.

She was watching Andreas dance with a rather lovely dark-haired creature whose name she could not recall. He was relaxed, smiling, and looked a completely different man from the one she was used to seeing. More the urbane man of sophistication, enjoying being with his own kind, she thought.

Then a smooth-as-silk voice drawled lightly beside her, 'Have you worked out yet which one is his mistress?'

Mistress? Claire struggled to keep her expression from altering, but the sickening squirm that suddenly hit her stomach sent some of the warmth draining from her cheeks.

Desmona saw it happen. 'You didn't know,' she sighed. 'Oh, how tragic for you—and on your betrothal night, too. I am so sorry...'

No, you're not, you're enjoying yourself, Claire silently contended, aware that she was being baited by a woman who—as Andreas had warned her—was out for her blood.

'He doesn't have a mistress.' She coldly dismissed the suggestion, but in reality she found herself suddenly having to face the fact that he most probably did have one somewhere. A man like Andreas would not put himself in a marriage of convenience without having that side of his needs adequately covered—surely!

'All Greek men of class have mistresses, darling,'

Desmona drawled deridingly. 'You could almost say it is expected of them. So, which one do you think?' she prompted. 'The lovely thing he is dancing with? Or the other one over there who can't take her eyes off him—or maybe the one standing in the corner, who looks too besotted with her husband to even notice Andreas.'

Without wanting them to, Claire's eyes flicked from woman to woman as Desmona pointed them out to her. And all of them—all of them were so beautiful that she wouldn't have blamed him for wanting any of them.

'I would go for the besotted one if I were you,' Desmona advised, not missing a single telling flicker of Claire's blue eyes. 'For the way she is clinging to her husband smacks of desperation to me...'

'I think you're lying,' Claire responded, refusing to let the other woman get to her.

'Then you are a fool,' Desmona replied. 'And maybe you deserve all you are about to receive from Andreas Markopoulou. For he may have good reason to want your child, but I cannot believe that he truly wants you—though he is cold-blooded and ruthless enough to take you if that is the only way he can achieve his aim. There,' she concluded. 'I have said what I needed to say. So now I will leave you to enjoy the rest of your betrothal party. Good luck, Miss Stenson.' She smiled as she turned away. 'I think you may well need it very soon...'

But why had she said it? Claire wondered as she watched Desmona walk smoothly away. To hurt her—Claire—or to hurt Andreas because he had rejected her?

In the end it didn't matter, because now the seed had been planted Claire could feel herself looking at every female face with new suspicious eyes.

Andreas was no longer dancing but talking to the woman Desmona had described as besotted with her husband. Well, she observed, there was no sign of the husband now as she laughed with Andreas, with her big eyes shining up into his.

Was she his mistress?

It's none of your business! she told herself furiously.

But knowing that didn't stop her from studying their body language as Andreas touched a light finger to the woman's shoulder, to her cheek, laughed softly at something she said to him and kissed the hand she used to teasingly cover his mouth when he gave what must have been a wicked reply.

The woman spoke again, only this time her expression turned very serious. With her hand still resting in his, Andreas sobered also, then began glancing furtively around them before giving a grim nod of his head. Then, turning, they moved off into one of the other rooms.

Even with that quick glance around to check that their withdrawal would not be observed, he didn't even notice me, Claire noted painfully. Then she saw Desmona's gaze fixed mockingly on her, and humiliation swept over her in a sickening wave.

It was one thing to deceive but quite another to *be* deceived, she realised, hurt, so very hurt that she didn't quite know what to do with herself as she stood there alone and feeling utterly unable to pretend it hadn't happened.

So when several of the younger guests approached her to say they had set up a disco outside on the pool terrace, then warily asked if she would like to join them, she was so relieved at the diversion from her own hectic thoughts that she accepted eagerly.

Half an hour later she was a different person. A person her mother would have recognised if she'd been there to see the old laughing, teasing, fun-loving Claire who danced disco with enthusiasm rather than stuffy waltzes with reluctance.

If there was something rather desperate about the way she threw herself into the fun, then no one seemed to notice that. They were just pleased to discover that Andreas Markopoulou's newly betrothed was nothing like the hard-crusted English floozy they had all been led to believe she would be.

Someone appeared with a case of champagne they'd pinched from somewhere. And for the next few minutes the small group threw themselves into the fun of making corks explode from bottles then quickly supping at the frothy wine as it spilled over the bottle rim.

After that the wine flowed like water, and as the intoxicating bubbles entered her bloodstream Claire began to let go of what was left of her inhibitions. The music was throbbing—and she danced like a dream. There wasn't one person there who didn't pause to take note of that as her long, slender body swayed and gyrated inside the slinky dress, with the kind of innate sensuality that made the other girls envious and the young men throb to an entirely different beat.

One young man who was bolder than the rest stepped up behind her to slide his hands around her silk-tulle-lined stomach and began gyrating with her. Claire laughed and didn't push him away; instead she began exaggerating her movements to which he had to follow.

'You are wasted on Andreas,' he whispered against her ear. 'He is too cold and stuffy for a wonderful creature like you.'

'I adore him,' Claire lied glibly, when really at that moment she was hating him so badly that she could barely cope with it. 'He's absolute dynamite.'

Not so big a lie, she acknowledged bleakly from some darker place inside her that she refused to go off to. Instead she turned her head against her shoulder and smiled a stunning smile into her new consort's captivated face.

That was how Andreas came upon her. He stopped dead in his tracks. 'Enjoying yourselves?' his deep voice harshly intruded, and effectively silenced the whole group in the blink of an eyelid as heads came up, twisted round, then simply froze to stare at him like guilty thieves caught red-handed.

He was standing in a circle of light being thrown from the open French window that led to the indoor pool just behind him. And even with his dark face cast in shadows there wasn't one of them present who didn't know that he was furiously angry.

Someone had the presence of mind to switch off the throbbing music. Then the silence that followed was truly stunning as he began striding forward.

His hard eyes were on Claire—and specifically fixed on the place where her companion's hands were splayed across her slender body.

Andreas didn't so much as glance at him, but with a sharp click of his fingers he had the young man snatching his hands away from her waist then stepping right back as if he was letting go of some stolen hot property.

Coming to an abrupt halt in front of Claire, Andreas reached out to take the champagne bottle she hadn't even been aware of holding out of her fingers. Then he stood there, impressively daunting, as he held the bottle out to the side in a grimly silent command for someone to take it from him.

Some very brave person did that, for the angry vibrations Andreas was giving off were frighteningly awesome. 'Now you may all return to the party,' he said flatly. And not once—not *once* had he so much as acknowledged a single one of them by eye contact!

Not even Claire, who was standing there rather like a puppet that had had its strings removed while the group responded to his command without a single murmur, disappearing *en masse* through the pool-house doors and effectively leaving her to face the angry wolf alone.

Thanks a bunch, she thought ruefully as she listened to their retreating footsteps fade away.

'Well, that was very sociable of you,' she drawled in an effort to mock her own tingling sense of trepidation at his continuing grim silence.

He didn't even bother to retaliate. All he did do was reach down to snatch up her only good wrist then turned and began pulling her towards the house.

'What do you think you are doing?' Claire demanded, trying to tug free of a grip that wouldn't budge.

'You are drunk,' he answered scathingly. 'I have no tolerance with that, so if you value your life you will be silent.'

'I am not drunk!' She hotly denied the charge—though she had a vague feeling he could well be right. 'Where are we going?' she then queried frowningly when, as they entered the indoor pool-room, instead of making for the door which would lead back to the main part of the house, he headed for the private staircase that connected the pool-room to the upper floor.

He didn't answer, but his body language did as he pulled her behind him up the stairs. He was blisteringly, furiously angry.

They emerged onto the upper landing. Below them the party was continuing in full swing. The hallway was crowded with people dancing, others spilling out from adjoining rooms. Peering over the gallery as they walked along it, the first person Claire's eyes picked out was Desmona's choice for Andreas's mistress, dancing cheek to cheek with her husband to the slow, smoochy music drifting sensuously in the air.

Two-timer, she thought contemptuously. And flashed the man in front of her a lethal glance.

He opened the door to her bedroom and swung her inside. Only a single small table lamp burned in the corner, casting eerie dark shadows over the rest of the room.

'Now,' he said, shutting the door, 'you are going to pull yourself together and make yourself fit to be seen with me when we return downstairs to our guests.'

'I was *with* our guests,' she threw back. 'And we *were* enjoying ourselves until you came and spoiled it!'

'You mean you enjoyed having that boy paw you?'

A sudden vision of his naked body wrapped around that adulterous woman downstairs had her chin coming up in hot defiance. 'What's it to you if I enjoyed it?' she challenged insolently. 'I don't recall either of us making any vows of celibacy when we decided to deceive everyone!'

His eyes narrowed dangerously. 'Explain that remark.'

Go to hell, she wanted to say, but those narrowed eyes stopped her. 'Let go of me,' she said instead, and tried to pull her wrist away.

He wouldn't let go. 'I said explain,' he repeated.

'What do you think I meant?' she flashed, hugging insolence around her like a protective shield. 'If you think I am going to sit here through this marriage like the ever faithful Penelope while you go off doing your own thing—then you can think again!'

The atmosphere between them was suddenly electric. He wasn't a fool; he knew exactly what she was saying here. If it were possible his eyes narrowed even more. Her blood began to fizz—not with champagne bubbles any more but with a far more volatile substance. Her heart began to pound, the muscles in her stomach coiling tensely as, in sheer self-preservation, she gave a hard yank at her imprisoned wrist and managed at last to break herself free then began edging backwards, attempting to put some much needed distance between them.

But he followed. 'You are not taking a lover while you are married to me,' he warned in the kind of deadly voice that put goose bumps on her flesh.

'You can't dictate to me like that,' Claire protested as she fell back another step—then another, until the backs of her trembling knees hit the edge of the bed. 'I can do whatever I want to do. You promised me that,' she reminded him. 'When I agreed to all of this.'

'And you want to take a lover,' he breathed in taut understanding.

'Why—will you be jealous?' she taunted him, with a sense of horror at her own crazy recklessness.

Something came alive on his lean, dark face that had her

hand shooting up to press against his chest in a purely defensive action meant to keep him back.

'No,' she murmured unsteadily. 'I didn't mean that.'

He said nothing, but his eyes were certainly talking to her. They were gazing down at the hectic heave of her breasts beneath the stretch-silk tulle as if he could actually see this so-called lover's hands on her body. And at last the alarm bells began ringing inside her head, warning her that she had finally managed to awaken the sleeping devil she'd always known must live somewhere inside him.

She should leave, she knew that. She should get the hell out of this bedroom and hide away somewhere until he had got his temper back.

But she didn't move another muscle. Instead she just stood there and trembled and shook.

A little whimper escaped her.

It was enough to bring his eyes flicking up to clash with her eyes—and their darkness was so blisteringly intense that her lungs suddenly stopped working altogether.

He was faring no better, she realised. His heart was pounding; she could feel it hammering against his ribs beneath the place where her hand lay flat against his chest in its puny effort to ward him off. He felt warm and tough, the masculine formation of well developed muscle so intensely exciting to her that she froze on a wave of horrified shock.

'No,' she breathed in shaken rejection—and went to jerk her hand away from him—only he stopped her by covering it with his own hand.

It was then that the heat went racing through her. The heat of fear, the heat of desire, the heat of a terrible temptation.

But what was worse was she could feel the self-same temptation thundering through him! He was still, he was tense, and he was vibrating with a desire so strong that there really was no denying it.

Anxious eyes flicked back to clash with his. 'No,' she repeated in breathless denial of what she saw written there. 'You don't want me,' she whispered shakily.

To her surprise he laughed, the sound so harsh and tight and bitterly deriding that it managed to make her wince. Yet she received the disturbing impression that it was himself he was deriding.

'You fool,' he muttered then, and before she could even feed the words into her brain he had spread one set of long brown fingers across the satin-smooth skin between her shoulder blades, cupped the other to the back of her head. And, with a hard, rough, angrily masculine jerk, he tugged her up against him then took her startled mouth hotly and savagely.

CHAPTER EIGHT

SHE didn't stand a single chance.

Her senses went haywire, every one of them making a mad scrambling surge towards that life-giving mouth like butterflies set free from the bonds of their chrysalis. Her lips fell apart, her tongue going in urgent search of its partner. He shuddered violently at the intimate contact, his hands banding her more closely to him. Like two magnets of opposing poles, they became locked together in a sizzling exchange that left no room for anything but the burning eruption that was taking place between them.

It was wild and it was hot, fuelled by his anger and her refusal to back down no matter what the consequences. It was a lethal combination that flung the whole thing spinning out of control so quickly that neither was able to snatch sanity back.

He took her mouth savagely—and savagely she replied, inciting the whole crazed, potent experience into a frenzy of desire that closed down time and space to this one small zone filled with a vibrant, soaring, passionate energy.

It was devouring—intoxicating. The more he took, the more she gave, arching to the stroke of his hands on her body, literally sighing with pleasure when he touched her breasts. Her injured hand was locked around his neck so her fingers could cling to his hair, her other hand lost inside his jacket, greedily learning every muscle-rippling contour along his back-bone as he jerked and shuddered to her touch.

It was like touching heaven, and if the door to the bedroom had suddenly swung open neither of them would have heard it, they were so lost, so caught up in a conflagration that had been sharply building between them for days.

'Claire...' He groaned her name against her hungry mouth.

Whether in pleasure or in protest she didn't know, but the sudden flare of heat coming from him set her own flesh burning. She gasped when she felt the power of his arousal surge against her. It caused an echoing eruption within herself, locking her thighs in an urgent need to maintain that vital contact as a flare of bright, blinding, blistering desire went shooting through her.

Like seasoned lovers, she thought dazedly. You would be forgiven for thinking that we did this with each other all the time! When in actual fact Claire had never felt like this before—ever!

The halter-style bodice to her dress dropped to her waistline, his hands feathered over newly exposed flesh, and she gasped on a tremor of nerve-tingling pleasure as her knees gave out and she toppled dizzily back onto the bed.

He followed her downwards so that they landed in a tangle of limbs that only seemed to intensify their excitement. His breathing was fast, his expression intense, his mouth still moist from their long, hot kiss. But it was the look in his eyes that sent Claire completely still beneath him.

In all her life, she had never seen anything like it before. It was hot and it was ravenous but it was also painfully—painfully vulnerable.

'I want you,' he said hoarsely.

'Yes,' she whispered. 'I can tell that you do.' But it was said very gently. For some reason that she didn't understand this big, strong, very arrogant man was hurting enough without her adding to it by taunting him.

Without really having to think about the wiseness of it, she reached up and kissed him—as a lover would kiss a true lover.

Then it was back. The hot, hard, driving passion that had no time or room for gentleness or leisure. He kissed like a man who hadn't done this for centuries, and she responded with a passion that she'd never known she possessed.

Her dress slid away without her even noticing, then his jacket, his shirt and tie. He kissed and licked and caressed and suckled her until she was so lost in the frenzied storm that she had no idea what she was doing any more.

So when she dared to fold her hand around the length of his burgeoning sex it came as a shock to feel him go utterly motionless beside her. Opening heavy, love-glazed eyes, she lay there watching as he seemed to take an actual pause in life itself. His eyes were closed, his dark face taut, his mouth flattened into a single white-ringed line of unbearable tension.

Yet not sexual tension, but a different tension.

'Andreas?' she breathed, unsure what was happening.

When he didn't respond she went to take her hand away, a hot flush of mortification staining her cheeks. But his hand snaked down to stay her, long fingers trembling slightly as they kept hers tightly wrapped around him.

Then he let the air out of his lungs in a long, slow, measured way, and his eyes fluttered open, revealing those dark, dark irises where that awful, wretched, pained vulnerability was back again.

He didn't say anything, though, and when he came to lean over her the tempo changed—the man changed, turning from ravaging hunter into devastatingly rich and sensual lover.

Still greedy, he was greedy—but then, so was she. She couldn't get enough of him, her teeth biting deeply into powerfully bunched muscle, her lips and tongue hungry to taste, to acquaint herself with this body that was giving her such untold pleasure.

It was as if nothing else in the world existed but each other. The party, the people, the anger—everything had been cast aside for this soul-filling journey into sensuality. He was heavy on top of her but she didn't care; her long and slender legs were parted while his hips thrust softly against her.

He wasn't inside her yet—but the experience was magical, the expression on his dark face so deeply intense that her heart swelled in her breast with a joy she could barely cope with.

I do love you so, she wanted to whisper. But just didn't dare in case she spoiled the magic.

So she did the next best thing and parted her legs that bit wider, smiled provocatively into the dark beauty of his impassioned face, arched her spine towards him—and invited him inside her.

His response was stunning. His dark face grew taut, his eyelids drooping over what she'd glimpsed as a flare of unbelievable emotion. Then, with a shudder that seemed to rip right through him, he buried himself in the deep, dark liquid heat of her body.

The small sting of pain she experienced at his entry barely registered, his short pause when he realised just what he had taken from her an acknowledgement of his prize. Then the passion coiled its hot, needy talons around them again, and the moment was forgotten—for the time being anyway.

No one said that making love had to be an earth-shattering experience. Only the lucky few reached those kind of peaks time after time.

They reached those peaks—surpassed them, rose onwards to another place where reality was suspended and the senses took over. When she began to flip over into that final climactic finish, Andreas wrapped her tightly to him, binding her there with his arms. Then, with each new measured thrust of his body, he watched as she shattered just that little bit more for him, her soft sounds of pleasure growing in strength, in volume, in vigour.

A sob broke from her—not a gasp, but a wild, bright electric sob of surrender that shook her body and kept on shaking it. And on a rasping growl he too surrendered to his own needs with driving thrusts that shattered what was left of both of them.

Coming down to earth again afterwards took a long, long

time, Claire discovered as she felt herself drifting gently through layer upon layer of sweet sensual fulfilment.

When she did eventually find the strength to take a small peek at reality, she found Andreas still lying heavy on her with his face pressed up against her throat, and his heart thundering against her breast.

He was still inside her. She could feel the exotic fullness of his manhood pulsing against the walls of her newly sensitised sex. It was wonderful. From hurt to anger to a blistering passion to this, she listed—this exquisite sense of supine contentment.

For the first time in months—maybe even years—she felt true happiness flood through her. 'I'm in heaven,' she whispered.

Andreas jerked away from her as if she were a poisonous snake. Taken by surprise by his abrupt withdrawal, her eyes flicked open to watch, in a state of bewildering confusion, him not only withdraw from her body but jackknife to his feet.

But worse than that was the expression on his face as he did it. He looked utterly devastated. Big and strong and godlike as he was in his full naked glory, when his eyes clashed briefly with her startled eyes he actually shuddered, his dark head wrenching to one side as if he couldn't bear to so much as look at her.

Hurt quivered through her, forcing her to sit up and hug her knees protectively to her chest. 'What?' she whispered shakily.

'No,' she thought she heard him utter, though even that single word was almost quashed in the way he swallowed thickly. 'This should not have happened,' he tagged on hoarsely.

What did he mean—it shouldn't have happened? Claire wondered painfully. 'Well, it just did!' she cried, her blue eyes dark pools of anger and hurt at his cruel insensitivity.

He didn't even acknowledge she'd spoken—couldn't even bring himself to look at her again!

Instead he just turned and strode quickly towards his own room, wrenched open the connecting door then disappeared through it—leaving Claire staring after him, white-faced and with her flesh chilling in mind-stunning dismay.

It should not have happened...

Still sitting there long, lost minutes later, huddled over her own bent knees in the middle of a sea of tumbled white bedding, Claire was bitterly agreeing with him.

For if it hadn't happened, then she would not have had to be sitting here feeling so painfully used then ruthlessly rejected.

Or punished would probably be a better word, she thought dully as she listened to him dressing somewhere in his own bedroom. She had also sat here suffering the sounds of him showering her scent from his flesh, because in his eagerness to get away from her he had forgotten to shut the connecting door and it stood half open, allowing her a blow-by-blow account of his every movement.

She shuddered sickeningly. Hating him, despising herself. Her first love, her first lover, and now this terrible feeling of hurt and rejection.

It should not have happened...

She had a horrible feeling that those words were branded in fire onto her very soul for ever now.

She should have run when her instincts had told her to. How could she have lost control like that and let him do what he had done?

Great to work that out in retrospect, she mused bitterly.

'I am going back down to our guests,' a deep voice informed her from the connecting doorway.

Claire didn't even lift her head up. She felt soiled and tainted, and unbearably humiliated.

'I suggest you remain here,' he went on stiffly. 'I will

make your excuses for you, blame your early retirement on your recent accident, or bridal nerves or—something. Are you all right?' he then tagged on with enough clear reluctance to make her wince.

'I'm not going to be a bride,' she mumbled from the confines of the white sheet she had pulled around her. 'The wedding is off.'

'Don't be foolish,' he sighed.

Why does he always call me foolish when I am at my most sensible? 'I want to go home to England tomorrow,' she insisted. 'And I never want to set eyes on you again.'

A small silence followed that, then another sigh to precede a rasping 'Look—I'm sorry' that sounded tense and uncomfortable and just damned bloody irritable.

No grace in that apology, she noted acidly.

'It was entirely my fault and I am now thoroughly ashamed of myself. Does that make you feel better?'

To know you're ashamed? 'No, it does not!' she cried, lifting flashing blue eyes to find him standing there looking as if he'd never been out of those clothes all evening.

When in actual fact what he had done was simply replace the first lot with the same again from his wardrobe because the ones he'd been wearing earlier were still lying in a crumpled heap on the carpet by her bed where they'd landed after being wrenched off him.

Self-contempt rippled through her as she saw herself eagerly helping him to remove them. She shuddered again, and drew the sheet more closely around her.

'Just go away, will you?' she choked, realised the tears weren't far away, and swallowed angrily down on them. For she wouldn't cry in front of this man ever again! she vowed fiercely.

He went to say something, but a raucous laugh filtered into the room from the galleried hallway below, and whatever he had been going to say turned into a heavy, 'I have to go back down there. We don't have time to deal with this now.'

I don't want to deal with it at all! Claire thought wretchedly. 'I bet they all know by now how you dragged me up here,' she whispered as humiliation sank its teeth deeper into her. 'I'll be the running joke of the party by now. Have you any idea how that makes me feel?'

'Don't,' he said tautly.

Don't what? she wondered. Don't hurt, don't feel used and humiliated—when she had every right to feel all of those things?

'I hate you,' she whispered, feeling the threatening tears burn all the hotter in her throat. 'The deal is off. So instead of lying you may as well go and give them that little piece of juicy truth to joke about!'

Suddenly he wasn't looking so good either, she noted. Despite the clean skin and the fresh suit of clothes, his skin wore the pallor of a man who still was not comfortable with himself.

But his words didn't sound anything but grimly resolute. 'I'm afraid I can't do that,' he refused. 'Things have gone too far for you to pull out of our arrangement now.'

'I was not aware that I was giving you a choice here!' she responded.

'And I am not giving you the choice to pull out,' he coldly shot back as he began walking towards her.

And—surprise, surprise! Claire mocked herself caustically—the ice was back like the loyal little friend it had always been to him!

'So listen to me, Claire, because I mean what I say…' He arrived by the bed, his tone deep with warning.

She buried her face in her knees again because she just couldn't bear to look him in the face this close to. He sighed harshly as if he knew exactly why she was hiding away like that.

'Our arrangement still stands as formerly agreed,' he grimly insisted, sounding insultingly as though he were chairing a business meeting. 'And although I know this development has—complicated things between us slightly nothing has really changed.'

Nothing has changed? What about me? Claire wanted to yell at him. What about the wretched change you've brought about in me? 'If you don't stop talking to me like a damned computer, I am likely to start screaming,' she breathed in seething fury.

He swung away from her—then back again, the action seeming to ignite his own fury. 'For the love of God, Claire!' he rasped. 'I am trying my best to be sensible amongst all of this—'

'Carnage,' she supplied for him when he bit back whatever choice of word he had been going to offer.

'Yes,' he hissed, seeming to accept that this was indeed carnage—which only made her hurt all the harder. 'But I can absolutely assure you this is not going to happen again. So we will go on as agreed. The marriage of convenience stands. I will take Melanie as my daughter. And you will still be free to get on with your own life unhindered by me just as soon as you are ready to. But if you think,' he then added very seriously, 'that I am going to let you break my grand-mother's heart in her final days, by walking away from our deal, then you are heading for trouble. For I don't take defeat on the chin like a gentleman. I fight back and I fight dirty.'

He meant it, too. Claire could hear the ruthless ice of intent threading every single word. She shivered; he saw it happen and seemed to take that as a gesture of acquiescence because he stepped back from the bed.

'Now I am going downstairs,' he announced less harshly—trying, Claire assumed, to defuse the tension simmering between them now he had made his point. 'Where I will make a very Greek joke about temperamental females with more spirit than any poor mortal male could possibly hope to deal with. And I will see you again in the morning.'

As he walked towards her door, Claire lifted her head to watch him leave with bitterness in her eyes. He turned unexpectedly, catching her looking at him, and she was trapped, caught by a pair of devil-black eyes that held knowledge of her no one else did. It hurt her, knowing that he now knew her so very intimately while she still felt she didn't know him at all, even after what they had just done to each other here in this bed.

'Will you be all right?' he questioned huskily.

'Yes,' she nodded, and wished he would just hurry up and go so she could curl up and weep her heart out.

Yet still he lingered with those dark eyes flickering restlessly over her. 'Shall I send Althea up to help you—do whatever it is you need her for?' he then offered, wafting a descriptive finger at her plaster-cast.

'I can manage.' She quietly refused the offer.

He nodded and turned back to the door then opened it while Claire held her breath in suffocating anticipation of his finally getting out of here.

But almost immediately he changed his mind and closed the door, though he did not turn to face her again. Stiff, tense, almost pompous in his delivery, he then had the gall to murmur gruffly, 'I would hate you to think that I do not appreciate the—honour you bestowed on me tonight. It was—'

'Will you just go?' Claire coldly interrupted, not wanting to know what *it* was.

He nodded, taking the hint. And this time when the door opened and closed again he was on the other side of it.

And at last Claire could do what she wanted to do, which was curl up in a tight ball on her side and sob her wretched heart out.

After the storm was over, she made herself get up, tape a plastic bag to her plaster-cast, then stood beneath the shower for long minutes, simply letting the heated sting of the water wash away the lingering pangs of emotion the tears hadn't cried away.

After putting on one of her new silk nightdresses, she began picking up his clothes and folding them neatly before taking them through to his room, reasonably sure she was not going to walk in on him.

Like her own room, his was lit by only a single small lamp left burning on the bedside table. In fact, in almost every way the room was a match to hers, she noticed—except his bed didn't look as if war had taken place in it, she thought with a small shudder as she laid the clothes down on the smooth pale grey counterpane then walked back into her own room to eye with distaste her tumbled bed.

An honour, he had called it. She called it a waste of something so very precious and she knew there was no way she could sleep in this bed again tonight.

Tears back and burning, with an angry jerk, she turned away from the wretched bed and walked across the room to the soft-cushioned sofa, where she curled herself up, then closed her eyes tightly in a grimly determined effort to shut the last dreadful hour right out of her head.

Surprisingly she slept, though she hadn't really expected to be able to switch her mind off as easily as that. Moreover, she slept long and heavily, and awoke the next morning vaguely aware of half surfacing only once during the night when she'd been dreaming that she was being carried.

It had been a disturbing sensation. Strangely painful though not in a physical way, she recalled as she lay there watching the morning sunlight draw patterns on the ceiling via the white voile drapes covering the windows.

'Don't cry,' an unbelievably gentle voice echoed inside her head.

Recognising that voice, she sat up with a start, saw she was back in her bed and knew exactly how she'd got there. It had been no dream last night! Andreas had come into her room and found her asleep on the sofa! He'd woken her up when he'd gathered her into his arms to carry her back to bed, and she even remembered the raw humiliation in starting to cry all over again!

Oh, how could you, Claire? she chided herself furiously. How could you let him see how hurt you are?

And there was worse—much worse, she recalled, closing her eyes in the hopes of shutting it all out again. But it would not be shut out. And she saw herself clinging to him. Saw him lay her gently on the bed then come down to lie beside her. She felt the light brush of his lips on her cheek and the way his hands had stroked her, quietly soothing her back into oblivion before he must have got up and placed the covers over her.

I hate him, she thought angrily. I really, really hate him for catching me out like that!

Too angry to just sit there tormenting herself, she got up and dressed quickly, needing to soothe her savaged ego by spending some time with Melanie.

She could even make herself a drink there, since the nursery came with its own fully equipped kitchen, which would save her having to face Andreas across the breakfast table.

The idea lifted her spirits, and as her brain fed that inspired thought to her stomach she realised just how desperate she was for some food and a hot cup of tea.

Dressed comfortably in a sage-green tee shirt and a pair of slim-fitting yellow Capri pants, she stepped out of her room to be immediately struck by how quiet the rest of the house was.

Early though she knew it was, she had expected the house to be a hive of activity by now as the staff cleared up after last night's party. But as she peered over the gallery rail at the huge hallway below she saw that the place had already been wiped clean of all evidence of partying.

The staff must have been working until the early hours, she realised, leaving them at liberty to have a well-earned lie-in this morning which probably meant that she was the only person up and around.

A prospect that suited her very well while she was still struggling to deal with what had happened last night, and she resolved to use their long day yesterday as an excuse for them to leave her to take care of Melanie today.

The nursery would give her somewhere to hide. Somewhere to lick her wounds and try to come to a decision as to what she was going to do. For the impulse to just pick up the baby and run before she dug herself even deeper into the mire her emotions were in was a gnawing ache that filled her brain.

If it hadn't been for Andreas's grandmother, she had a suspicion she would have done it already and stolen away in the dead of night like a thief running off with the family silver.

Also there was still Melanie to consider. Melanie who could gain so much from living this kind of luxury life—and so little from the life Claire could give her.

Not many pluses in favour of running, she heavily concluded, and she hadn't even taken into consideration the dire threat of retribution Andreas had laid on her last night.

Inside the nursery all was quiet, the early morning sunlight diffused by the pretty apple-green curtains still drawn across the windows. Claire quietly closed the door behind her, and was about to walk over to the crib to check on the baby when a sound in the other corner of the room had her head twisting round, expecting to see Althea—only to freeze when she found herself looking at Andreas.

Dressed in what looked like a white cotton tracksuit, he was sitting in the comfortable rocking-chair in the corner, cradling a sleeping Melanie in his arms.

His eyes were closed, his dark head resting back against the chair's cushioned back—though he wasn't asleep. The way one long brown bare foot was rhythmically keeping the chair rocking while the other rested across its knee told her that.

He was just too lost within his own deep train of thought to have heard her arrival.

Not pleasant thoughts either, she noticed, looking at the

grim tension circling his shadowy mouth. Then she had to
suffer a vivid action replay of what that mouth had made her
feel like last night and she unfroze with a jolt, her first instinct to turn and leave quickly before he realised she was
there.

His eyes flicked open, catching her in the act of a cowardly
retreat. The chair stopped rocking. They both froze this time.
The fact that Andreas was as disconcerted to find her standing there as she was to find him was enough to hold them
trapped as a new knowledge of each other raked through the
silence in a whiplash so painful it seemed to strip Claire's
tangled emotions bare.

Neither spoke; neither seemed able to. Her heart was
pounding, her throat thickening up on a stress overload that
was seriously affecting her ability to breathe.

What he was feeling was difficult to define with a man so
good at keeping his own counsel, but something stirred in
the unfathomable black eyes.

Regret, she wondered, or even remorse? Whatever it was
it managed to hurt a very raw and vulnerable part of her, and
she would have continued her cowardly retreat if he hadn't
spoken.

Speaking softly so as not to awaken the baby, he said,
'Kalimera…' offering her the Greek morning greeting that
she had grown very used to over the last few days.

Slowly she turned back to him. 'Kal-Kalimera,' she replied
politely, not quite focusing on him.

'You are up early. It is barely six o'clock,' he remarked,
trying, she knew, to sound perfectly normal but it was a strain
and it showed in the slight husky quality of his voice.

She nodded, licked her dry lips and wished her heart would
stop racing. 'S-so are you,' she managed, but that was all she
could do.

'I haven't been to bed,' he replied, glancing ruefully at the
baby. 'Melanie has had a disturbed night. Althea was exhausted so I sent her to bed around dawn and took over here.'

'Oh!' Instant concern for Melanie had her moving towards him on legs that were trembling with nervous tension. 'Someone should have come for me!' she protested as she peered worriedly at the baby.

'I was here.' That was all he said, yet it seemed to say it all. For he handled the baby girl as if he had been doing it all her little life. It was, in fact, the talk of the house how good he was with the baby. Claire already knew he spent time with her sister every morning before he left for Athens, and the same in the evening when he got home again.

Bonding was the modern term for it, and Claire supposed it described what Andreas had been doing since Melanie had arrived in his life.

'What has been the matter with her?' she asked now.

He smiled that brief smile—wry, though, not grim. 'I have been reliably informed by the experienced Lefka that babies do have restless nights.'

Claire nodded knowingly, her fingertips already stroking Melanie's cheek without even realising she was doing it. 'She hardly slept at all after Mother died,' she confided sadly. 'You wouldn't think someone so young could know, but I think she missed her dreadfully.'

'As you do?'

Her throat thickened at the gentle question. She answered it with another nod. 'I'll take her now, if you like,' she offered. 'Then you can go and get some rest...'

But even as she reached out to take the baby from him Andreas caught hold of her fingers.

The very fact that he was touching her was enough to bring the panic back. Her tension suddenly soared. Yet, though he had to feel it, he grimly ignored it. 'She is happy with us, Claire,' he said urgently. 'You must be able to see that?'

Which meant what? she wondered. That Melanie had never been happy with only her sister taking care of her?

As usual, he read her thoughts. 'No.' He renounced them. 'You misunderstand me. You have *both* been grieving—*both* of you, Claire. And although I know you may not be prepared to accept this right now you have *both* been happier in my care!'

She knew what he was saying. She knew *exactly* what it was he was getting at. He wanted her to agree to stay without him having to exert undue pressure on her. He wanted her to go on as before as if last night had never happened.

As if nothing had changed.

'Give this a chance,' he pleaded huskily. 'Give *me* a second chance to make this work for us—if only for Melanie's sake...'

For Melanie's sake. If this organ throbbing thickly in her breast was still a heart, she mused heavily, then she would have that phrase engraved on it.

I did this—for Melanie's sake.

She gave one last nod of her head in mute acquiescence.

It was enough. He let go of her fingers and silently offered her the baby. Melanie snuffled then settled into her arms. Andreas stood up, looking taller, leaner, darker in his all-white tracksuit. He was about to step around her so that she could sit down when he paused, touched her pale cheek with a gentle finger, and murmured, 'Thank you.'

Then he was gone, quickly, beating a hasty retreat now he had what he wanted.

Which wasn't Claire, she told herself in dull mockery.

CHAPTER NINE

IT WAS a retreat that had in fact taken him right out of the firing line, Claire discovered when she eventually emerged from the sanctuary of the nursery which had turned out to be no sanctuary at all in the end.

'A problem with one of his latest acquisitions,' she was told. But Claire knew the real problem was her and that he had simply taken himself away so as not to risk anything else going wrong before the wedding.

But then, she was his latest acquisition, she supposed. So she couldn't call the excuse a lie exactly.

The rest of that week slid by quickly. She spent the time sharing herself between Melanie and Andreas's grandmother, who was determined to make sure her precious grandson's bride walked down the aisle looking as perfect as she had looked herself all those many years ago.

She produced a wedding veil of the same heavy lace as the dress, and commanded Claire to put it on then presented her with two delicately worked diamond and gold hair combs which she then instructed her exactly where to position to hold the veil in place. Next day came the diamond necklace and earrings to match the ring Claire already wore on her finger.

'My husband gave me these the night before we married,' she said sighingly. And Claire didn't have the heart to protest at being given so many precious things to wear when the old woman's eyes looked so full of wonderful memories.

I'll hand them all back to Andreas straight after the wedding, she consoled her uneasy conscience. At least then I won't feel like a thief as well as a fraud.

After those uncomfortable visits she would steal her sister

and push her out in the gardens while she tried to re-convince herself that doing this was not so much deceiving a very old lady as trying her best to make her happy in her final days.

Sometimes it worked, sometimes it didn't, but having no Andreas around to bounce either feeling off meant she had to deal with the conscience-struck days herself.

So her wedding day arrived, and behind a protective haze of disassociation she went through with it, stepping into the tiny but beautiful candlelit church on the arm of Andreas's uncle Grigoris to be handed over to a man who had taken back the guise of tall, dark stranger in the days since she'd seen him last.

All those who had been at the betrothal party were here to watch them marry. Like a puppet responding to each pull on its strings, Claire repeated vows she didn't mean to a man who didn't mean them, his voice a dark and husky rumble that vibrated through her system like the growl of a hungry animal who saw her as its next meal.

Only this particular animal didn't really want to eat her. So that fanciful impression was just another deception she could add to a growing list of them.

A slender gold wedding band arrived on her finger. She was kissed—though she completely shut herself off from it. She caught a glimpse of his eyes, though, as he drew away again. They were narrowed and probing the strained whiteness of her face.

She looked away. That kind of intimate contact was just too much for her right now.

They arrived back at the house to find that the wedding breakfast was to take place outside on the lawn. But when she went to move in that direction, already armouring herself for the next ordeal of having to face again all those people who, in her mind, had somehow become indelibly linked with the night of her wretched leap into womanhood, Andreas stayed her with the light touch of his fingers on her shoulder.

Sensation ripped through her like a lightning bolt, straightening her spine and drawing the breath into her lungs on a stricken gasp.

Why it happened, when she had managed to disregard every other time he had touched her today, she didn't know.

But his fingers snapped back, his lean face freezing in what she could only believe was shock. 'I can accept it is a bride's right to look pale and interestingly ethereal,' he rasped out harshly. 'But do you think you could at least refrain from behaving as a lamb being led to her sacrifice?'

'Sorry,' she said awkwardly, but it was already too late for the apology.

He turned away from her, angry, tense. 'We have another ordeal to contend with before we can go out to greet our guests,' he then informed her grimly. 'My grandmother is waiting to meet Melanie.'

Of course, she thought as mutely she followed him towards the stairs. Melanie was no longer an illegitimate member of this family—which was the real point to all of this after all. So why hadn't she considered this eventuality?

Because it had been one lie that had become lost within all the other lies. She answered her own question.

The amber eyes flicked over Claire then did the same to Andreas, who was standing beside her holding Melanie. And Claire knew the old lady was superimposing her own and her late husband's image over the top of them as she did so.

'Perfect,' she sighed out in eventual satisfaction. 'Except for the child, of course,' she then added censoriously. 'I would have been banished from the family and my dear Tito would have been whipped to within an inch of his life. Now, get me that soft cushion over there,' she went on impatiently. 'Place it on my knee then let me have my great-granddaughter.'

Eager now—almost greedy in her desire to hold the baby, Claire moved to her bidding, collecting the requested cushion and laying it on the old lady's lap. With infinite care, Andreas followed it with Melanie, then they both straightened to watch as the bony fingers of her only useful hand gently touched Melanie's cap of silky black hair then stroked her baby cheek.

As if she sensed a stranger around, Melanie's eyes flicked open and stared directly into the wizened old face leaning over her. It was an electrifying moment, though Claire didn't know why it felt like that. But a few seconds later Andreas's grandmother lifted her eyes up to his, and static was suddenly sparking between them.

'You devil,' she said.

That brief grim smile of his appeared. 'And you are just too shrewd for your own good sometimes,' he replied.

Then they both went on speaking in their own language while Claire stood by, utterly lost to the conversation, though she was aware that it took the form of a very sharp question-and-answer session that seemed to be including her because the old lady kept on glancing sharply at her.

The inquisition was concluded with a final thoughtful glance in Claire's direction and a brief nod of her head. 'Now send Althea to me,' the old lady commanded, and her attention was back on the baby lying wide awake now on her lap. 'And leave me to get to know my great-granddaughter in peace.'

'What was all that about?' Claire dared to ask after they'd left his grandmother with Althea safely ensconced to watch over Melanie.

'She likes to think she still has control over everything, you know that,' he drawled dismissively.

'She called you a devil.' And she'd meant it, Claire thought frowningly.

'Maybe I am,' he replied in a light, mocking vein that nonetheless still made Claire feel that, like his grandmother, he was being serious.

She was missing something here; she knew she was; she just didn't know what the something was.

Then Andreas was diverting her thoughts into a whole new area that completely dismissed everything else for a while. Because he took her to his study and produced a set of legal documents that were, he explained, a formal application to the British authorities for them both to legally adopt Melanie.

Yet another stage of his carefully thought out game-plan, she mused bleakly as she set her signature to each page as Andreas indicated. A game-plan that had gone very smoothly for him—if you didn't count that one small glitch in the middle when he'd given in to his baser instincts and seduced one of the expendable pawns.

'Don't look so worried,' he said. 'This will strengthen your claim on Melanie, not weaken it. Trust me.'

Trust me... It was quite a request when she was already being plagued by a feeling that there were things going on here that she didn't know about.

But then, expendable pawns did not necessarily need to know the overall plan of the main player, did they? she mocked herself. Or was she just overreacting and reading too much into light, throw-away remarks that probably held no hidden agenda?

It suited her better to believe the latter when she still had one last ordeal to get through—namely playing the happy bride throughout the rest of that day—for her own pride's sake, because her pride needed to remedy the poor impression she had given of herself in front of these people the last time they'd been together like this.

Maybe Andreas was of a similar mind because he never left her side for a moment and played the attentive groom to the hilt. And slowly—slowly Claire began to feel comfortable with him again; she even laughed once or twice at some smoothly whispered remark he made in her ear about one of his relatives.

It was nice. She even discovered that she was actually enjoying herself.

As the day softened into evening, people relaxed at white-linen-covered tables with champagne glasses chinking and the light-hearted conversation eddying softly all around.

The stars came out. Several tall torches mounted on wrought-iron stakes that had been driven into the lawn were lit to add yet another dimension to the rather seductive scene. Then, to top it all, a group of musicians arrived and set up in a shadowy corner of the garden. Classical Greek music began filtering into the evening air.

Without a word, Andreas drew Claire to her feet and walked her over to the terrace then pulled her gently into his arms. Feeling shy and self-conscious when everyone turned to watch them, she looked down at her plastered wrist, which felt very cumbersome suddenly, and wondered flusteredly where she was supposed to rest it while they danced.

He solved the problem for her, by lifting it up and around his nape as he set them moving slowly to the music. It brought her too close to his body—reminded her of when she had last placed her arm around his neck like this—and she tensed up accordingly.

'Stop it,' he murmured softly. 'Don't spoil it.'

Don't spoil it… She reinforced that remark, and made herself relax, made herself ignore that warm, hard body brushing against her own as they moved. She made herself pretend that the butterflies were not going wild inside her stomach. And she refused to so much as flicker a fleeting glance at the shadowy mouth that only required her to raise her head a half inch for her own mouth to be in burning contact with it.

'You make an enchanting and very lovely bride, Claire,' his dark voice inserted into the silence between them. 'Some day some man is going to be very fortunate to claim you as his prize.'

But not you, she made bleak note, understanding exactly why he felt the need to say that. He was reinforcing *his* position just in case she might be dreaming of a more romantic ending while she danced with him like this.

'I'll look forward to it,' she replied, wishing that her response could cut him as deeply as his words had done to her.

If he reacted at all Claire never found out because at the same moment Lefka appeared at Andreas's elbow, the look on her face enough to warn them that something was dreadfully wrong. Bending towards the housekeeper, Andreas listened to what she murmured in his ear. And, as Claire had witnessed many times during the short period she had known him, she saw his expression completely freeze.

'What's wrong?' she demanded anxiously when Lekfa melted away again.

'One moment,' he said, no emotion, no warning of what was to come showing in his flattened voice as he glanced around the people present and eventually caught the eye of his uncle Grigoris. The older man came hurrying over. By then Claire was trembling, though she didn't know why.

Andreas murmured something to Grigoris in Greek. The older man's face dropped in dismay. 'Take care of my wife for me,' he then added in English. And, without making eye contact with her once since Lefka had come to him, he turned and disappeared into the house.

'Please…' She turned her anxiety on Grigoris. 'What's happened? Where has he gone? Is it Melanie?' she then added on a sudden jolt of maternal anguish.

Grigoris shook his steely head, his dark eyes—usually full of laughter—looking unbearably sad. 'It is Yaya,' he murmured huskily.

Then, while Claire stood frozen herself as realisation began to wash coldly through her, Grigoris placed a hand around her waist for support and turned to the rest of the party.

'Attend to me, everyone,' he announced. 'Yaya Eleni has gone. The party is now over…'

Dressed in a long aquamarine silk nightdress and a matching robe, Claire had fallen into a fitful doze on her bed when a sound in the room woke her.

Opening her eyes, she saw Andreas standing by the long French window that led out to the veranda. He had pulled back the voile drape and was staring out at the moon-kissed evening. His jacket and tie had gone and the sleeves were rolled up on his white shirt, his hands lost inside the pockets of his iron-grey trousers.

Lying there studying him, Claire felt her heart give a wrench in aching sympathy—because though his broad shoulders were straight and his spine erect he still managed to emit a mood of utter dejection.

'What time is it?' she asked, smothering a yawn behind a hand.

He glanced at her—then away again. 'Late,' he replied sombrely. 'Very late. Go back to sleep. I had no intention of disturbing you. I just did not want to—'

Be alone, Claire silently finished for him with the pained understanding of one who knew. 'I wasn't asleep,' she said. 'Just dozing.'

He nodded in acknowledgement but that was all, his concentration seemingly fixed on some far-away point way out on the horizon when she knew he wasn't seeing anything but the darkened shadow of his own grief.

Sliding her feet off the edge of the bed, she sat up then stood up, ignoring the protest of muscles that had been slaves to tension for too long that day as she went to stand beside him.

'Did she feel anything?' she questioned softly.

He released a short laugh that almost strangled into a choke. 'She died in her sleep with a smile on her face,' he replied very dryly.

'She went happily, then, as you wanted her to,' Claire pointed out. 'You have to take some consolation from that.'

'Do I?' He smiled that brief smile and Claire couldn't bear it because although he was staring directly ahead the moon-light shone on the moisture in his eyes.

Without thinking twice about what she was doing, she

slipped round in front of him, put her arms around him and laid her cheek against his chest. For if anyone needed physical contact with another human being right now, then it was him.

His first reaction was to stiffen at the unexpected gesture. Then, when he came to realise what she was offering him, he muttered gruffly, 'You are too wise for your age.'

'Age is not a prerequisite to feel what you're feeling,' she countered. 'Believe me, I've been there, so I know.'

His answer to that was a heavy sigh, then he relaxed a little, and his hands left his pockets to link loosely around her. 'Grigoris said you disappeared as soon as he had told everyone. Where did you go?'

'I hid in Melanie's room,' she confessed, lifting her face up to wrinkle her nose at him in acknowledgement of her own cowardice. 'I didn't think I could have coped with their pitying looks if I'd stayed there in my bridal finery, looking about as out of place as anyone could look.'

'You could have changed into something more—suitable,' he suggested, refusing to let her off the hook for her desertion.

'After all the trouble your grandmother went to, to re-create herself in me?' she protested. 'She would never have forgiven me!'

He smiled—he actually managed to smile! Claire began to feel dizzy at her success in teasing away his melancholy, even if it was only temporary.

'But you changed eventually,' he made wry note, sliding his thumbs against the silk of her robe at the base of her spine, sending a sprinkling of static washing through her.

She tried not to respond to it by concentrating all her attention on the remark. 'After you took her to the chapel,' she nodded. 'I felt she wouldn't mind if I changed then—don't ask me why,' she added wryly. 'Because I don't really understand it myself.'

'It does not need explaining, Claire,' he murmured very

softly. 'You honoured her passing in the way you thought she would appreciate it the most. I—thank you for that.'

'No need,' she shrugged, and began to ease herself away from him as the moment when she could excuse her closeness to him as comfort began to fade.

But he didn't let her go. Instead his loosely linked arms closed just that little bit tighter around her. And out of sheer desperation she spun in his arms to face the window, so he couldn't see the kind of control it was taking for her not to show what his touch was doing to her.

'You know, I won't hold you to your commitment to Melanie now that your grandmother is no longer here,' she told him.

'I thought you understood that I want that commitment,' he replied.

'Yes,' she nodded. 'But it is no longer necessary, is it?' If it was ever necessary, she added silently. She'd never really understood his motives where Melanie was concerned. 'Which seems to make a mockery of the whole thing.'

'Things stay as they are,' he decreed. 'And I would prefer not to have this conversation right now.'

'Oh, of course.' Instantly contrite for bringing it up when naturally he wanted to think only of his grandmother, she spun around in his arms to offer him a small smile of apology. 'Sorry,' she murmured. 'I just thought I would...'

'Let me off the hook,' he inserted for her. 'When it still does not seem to have sunk in with you that I have no intention of being let off—or to let you off it either,' he added pointedly.

'Well, a sham of a marriage seems a bit of a wasted gesture now.' She grimaced.

'When is a sham not a sham?' he pondered curiously.

Glancing up, Claire stopped breathing when she saw the dark gleam inside the hooded sombre eyes. He wants me, she realised. It's the reason why he came in here, why he broke the rules and crossed my threshold without first gaining my permission. He did not do it to talk about his grandmother but because he needs a woman to lose himself in tonight and that woman is me!

So, what are you going to do about that? she asked herself. But even as the question was filtering through her brain she was going up on tiptoe to brush her mouth against his.

His reply was a shaky sigh against the gentle pressure of her lips. 'What was that for?' he asked as she drew away again, trying to sound mocking and only managing to sound dreadfully needy.

'It's my wedding night,' Claire reminded him softly. 'And I want you. Will you make love to me, Andreas—please?'

Had she said it to protect his pride so he didn't have to lower it to ask her the same question? Claire wondered later. Or was it just that she was responding to her own needs?

Whichever it was, at least he didn't reject her—as she knew he was very capable of doing. Instead he released a muffled curse then was fiercely claiming her mouth.

Standing there with the moonlight shining in on them, he caressed and stroked and kissed the nightdress from her body, then stood back a little to sombrely rid himself of his own clothes.

He wasn't happy with himself for wanting her like this, and Claire wished she had the experience to remove his clothes for him in a way that would make him lose touch with himself, never mind his reservations. But she was no *femme fatale*, and with one near-useless hand she knew she wouldn't be able to pull it off with any grace. So she had to content herself with watching his moon-kissed, satiny flesh appear as his shirt was removed before he bent down to remove his shoes and socks.

Yet he stopped right there. Claire frowned at him as he reached for her again. 'You haven't finished,' she whispered.

'I will,' he promised. 'But later...'

Later turned out to be after he had carried her to the bed and laid her down on it. Later was when he had driven her into a mindless state of unbearable arousal that left not a single inch of her flesh untouched by his touch. Later was after she had driven him almost over the edge by trailing her mouth over his chest and had learned the intense pleasure in toying with a small, tight male nipple.

Later was when she had grown bold enough to move on downwards, utilising the expertise with which he had aroused her to arouse him. But when her sensual journey was halted by the waistband of his trousers he stopped her from taking them from him by pulling her beneath him, and, ignoring her small cry of protest at his frustrating tactics, he began the whole wildly erotic process of arousing her all over again.

So by the time his idea of later arrived she was so lost in the sensual haze he had created that she didn't even notice him ridding himself of the wretched trousers until he came over her and she felt the power of his naked arousal just before he pushed urgently inside her...

This time, it really should not have happened.

'Don't say anything,' she warned him.

She was sitting at Lefka's huge scrubbed kitchen table, hugging a mug of hot coffee in her hands as if her life depended on it. There was no colour in her face whatsoever, and her hair was a tangled mess around her shoulders, her body cloaked in a towelling bathrobe that covered her from neck to feet.

He, by contrast, was fully dressed in fresh trousers and a polo shirt. He looked neat, clean, perfectly presented. But then, he'd shot off into his bathroom so damned fast that he could have had ten showers before Claire had recovered enough to move!

After he had lifted his weight from her, of course— quickly, like the last time. Body still shuddering—like the last time.

'I—'

'I said don't!' she choked out.

The silence screamed. The tension, the bitterness. Like an action replay of last time.

Then he sighed and moved away, walking wearily across the kitchen. Checking the coffee-pot with his hand, he poured himself out a cup then came to sit down at the table.

Claire flicked him a glance. He was staring down at his drink and his shoulders were hunched over. The strain of the last twelve hours was so severe in his face now that he looked like a man who was having to carry the weight of the world on his shoulders.

She looked away before she started feeling sorry for him again. He might look like Atlas, but he isn't, she reminded herself brutally. He is just a man—an ordinary man with ordinary appetites. And an extraordinary way of dealing with the aftermath.

'Do you have a mistress?' she shot at him.

His head came up, dark eyes very guarded. 'What?' he murmured warily.

'Desmona did warn me that you had a mistress tucked away somewhere, but with everything else I forgot to ask. So I am asking you now.'

'Desmona said that?' He frowned. 'When?'

'At the betrothal thing.' She refused to call it a party. 'She pointed out a couple of candidates and suggested I choose.' Her eyes flicked up again, catching him without his guard, and his expression was—

She looked away again quickly, not wanting to acknowledge what that expression was telling her because it had the power to shatter the brand-new shell of protection she was hugging closely around her.

'You haven't answered the question,' she prompted huskily.

'There is no one,' he said.

Eyes fixed on her cup, she tried to decide if she could believe him when the man found it so easy to be economical with the truth.

'There is no one, Claire,' he repeated in the kind of tone that forced her to believe him. 'I would not do that to you. Desmona was talking like a loser, that was all.'

Which was what Claire had told herself when Desmona had fed her the poison, she remembered. 'Good,' she said, deciding to believe him. 'That means I have one less guilty sin to carry around with me.'

'What we did just now was not sinful,' he denied.

'No?' she mocked. 'Well, it certainly feels as if I've just done something dreadful.'

'We made love!' he husked.

'No—we had sex!' she burst out. 'Just the same as we did a week ago. W-we had sex, then you walked away—just like you did a week ago. And I f-feel unclean,' she added painfully. 'Just like I did a week ago.'

'I did not walk away from *you* just now,' he asserted heavily. 'I walked away from—'

The words stopped.

Sitting there with bated breath, Claire waited for him to continue. But he didn't. Instead he ran a tired hand through his perfectly combed hair—and added nothing.

'May you burn in hell,' she murmured succinctly.

To her surprise he laughed—albeit cynically. 'I have been burning away in that place for years,' he drawled with an irony that flew right by her. 'You will have to come up with a better curse than that to hurt me.'

And why do I get the impression that he knows exactly what that curse would be? she wondered, seeing a flash of something almost haunted pass across his eyes.

'Whatever,' she said, dismissing the look—because she had to do that if she was to remain strong. 'Burn in hell or laugh at it. It doesn't really matter to me. I don't want you to come near me like that ever again—do you hear?'

With that she got up with the intention of leaving him—but his next words stopped her. 'I'm sorry if I let you down,' he said very huskily. 'I didn't do it to hurt you, Claire. I just didn't think.'

'You mean—you always walk away from a woman directly after making love to her?' she asked derisively.

There was a distinct pause—more a guarded hesitation—before he sighed out, 'Yes.'

'The man on a mountain,' she murmured softly, aware that the cryptic remark would mean nothing to him. She shivered inwardly. 'I understand now. It's yourself you feel the need to walk away from.'

She had been throwing out words haphazardly with the specific need to hurt him, but as she stood there watching his face grow white beneath his olive skin before it closed up altogether Claire realised, with a small shock, that she had hit the nail right upon its head!

'You know me so well,' he drawled, offering her that grim brief smile again in an effort to cover his reaction up.

And she wanted to hit him—probably would have done if she hadn't noticed the tremor in his fingers as he reached for his cup. He was more affected by all of this than he wanted her to believe.

What was it with him, Claire wondered furiously, that he hated wanting her as a woman so much that he kept his wretched sexuality hidden inside his trousers until the very last moment? As if he had still been praying for deliverance right up until then, she realised with a shudder.

And on a muffled sob she turned and ran from the kitchen—kept on running, across the hall and up the stairs, desperately needing to get to her room before she broke down and wept.

Panting and sobbing together by the time she reached her bedroom, she barely had a chance to close the door before it was thrust open again.

'Go away!' she cried.

'Don't...' he groaned, reaching out to pull her into his arms.

To her horror she pressed her face into his chest and sobbed all the harder.

It wasn't fair! she told herself pitiably. He loved his grandmother. He could love Melanie. Why was it so terrible for him to try to love her?

His first wife, she then remembered with a sudden chilling of her flesh. She must have been quite something to have locked his heart up as totally as this.

Fighting for control of the tears now, she tried to push away from him.

'No,' he refused, his arms only tightening around her.

Her face lifted away from his chest, blue eyes awash with so many painful things that it was impossible to pick which was hurting her the most. 'Oh, please,' she pleaded helplessly. 'Please, Andreas, let me go.'

For some unfathomable reason, hearing her use his name in that pained, wretched way unlocked something desperate inside him. His chest expanded on a tense draw of air, his eyes flashing with some awful emotion—then he lowered his head and crushed her mouth to his with a hunger so fierce that it caught her utterly blindsided.

Once again Claire discovered that she didn't stand a chance. Not with emotions running as rife inside her as they were doing right now. And his mouth was hot, the taste of her own tears mingling with the moistness of his tongue. It was a seductive combination. The passion ignited like a fork of lightning that exploded to smithereens all hope of control. She didn't even notice when her robe fell apart, or hear his muffled curses as he struggled with the zip on his straining trousers.

He entered her with a thrust that brought him to his knees with her straddled across him with his hands clamped to her hipbones.

'Oh, dear God,' she groaned against his devouring mouth as her body went wild for him.

But he lost it first, shooting into her like a man experiencing his first release. He couldn't control it, could not control the gasping pants that shot from his pulsing body. When she joined him his grip on her hips was locked tight. And as she went limp against him he crumbled sideways, his arms shifting upwards to control her fall as they landed in a tangle of trembling limbs on the bedroom floor.

What now? Claire wondered as she reached rock-bottom of the slow slide back to wretched sanity. Another quick withdrawal followed by a walk-out? She even tensed herself in preparation for it.

'I'm still here.'

His voice sounded like gravel, vibrating against her cheek where he had her face pressed against him. He hadn't let go of her, and she was still lying with her limbs locked around him.

'I'm going nowhere.'

'Why not?' she whispered.

'You were right about me,' he said. 'I do prefer to stand alone. I don't find it easy to be open with my feelings. But— as God is my witness, Claire, I want you. I want *this* with you!' His arms tightened round her. 'And if that means I must change then I will damn well change!' he vowed. 'And I will start by holding you like this for as long as you want me to.'

He meant it—he really meant it! The tears came back, but she wasn't sure what they were for any more.

'Say something,' he prompted huskily, and she felt the tremor in his lips as they brushed her brow.

Say something, she repeated to herself. But what dared she say? Could she take a chance on this actually meaning something? The trouble was, she loved this man—had known that for quite a while now—while he seemed to only lust after her. How long did lust last? Especially with a man as self-contained as Andreas?

'I want to go to bed,' she said.

There was a short, sharp pause, then a heavy sigh as he went to get up.

'Your bed,' she added, lifting her face out of his shirt-front so she could look warily into his equally wary eyes. 'I want to sleep in your bed, in your arms all night and wake up still there in the morning,' she told him huskily.

'Then what?'

Claire gave a helpless little shrug. 'I don't know,' she answered honestly. 'What do you want?'

'You,' he said gruffly, then repeated it. 'I want you,'

Her poor heart fluttered, attempting to reach out and grab those words because they were the closest thing she'd had to a declaration of caring from him.

There was a short, sharp pause, then a heavy sigh at the
other end of the —

Your bed ... She pulled, flicking her face out at her every so ...
so she could lick out my into his equally way over ... I went
to sleep in your bed ... eyes clear, his head and walk up still
close to the morning, she was here in the

CHAPTER TEN

DEATH was a strange thing. It brought some people closer
together and pushed others wide apart. In Claire's own experience, she had lost more than a father when he'd passed
away; she'd also lost lifelong friends who could not deal with
the tragedy of the situation.

But when she stood beside Andreas as they buried his
grandmother she found herself being drawn closer to the last
person she would have expected, when Desmona suddenly
broke down and began weeping so desperately that Claire
didn't think twice about going over and gently placing her
arms around the other woman.

'You were very kind to her, considering the circumstances,' Andreas remarked much later as they were preparing for bed.

They shared a room now. They shared a life. Claire was
even daring to think that they were sharing a marriage.

'She needed someone,' she answered simply. 'It had never
occurred to me until Desmona broke down like that that she
and your grandmother must have been close.'

'Desmona has been a member of this family for many
years,' he reminded her. 'We all—care for her, though sometimes she makes it difficult to do so,' he added dryly.

'Is that why the family wanted you to marry her?' she
asked curiously. 'Because they care for her?'

'No.' He laughed, a softly mocking, sexily husky sound
that curled up her toes. 'Wanting me to marry Desmona was
an act of expediency. She owns rather large blocks of shares
in some of our most lucrative companies and they wanted to
keep them in the family.'

'But she is in love with you,' Claire pointed out. 'Or why would she agree to marry you?'

'Desmona loves Desmona,' he murmured sardonically. 'But she loves money even more. Marrying me would have given her relatively free access to the Markopoulou fortune once again. A very worthy cause in her eyes, believe me.'

'You're so cynical sometimes,' Claire sighed.

'Then reform me,' he invited, and covered her mouth, effectively ending the discussion when other, far more important things demanded her attention: mainly this man, who had become the centre of her universe so quickly that she didn't dare let herself consider just how deeply she had let herself fall in love with him.

So the next few weeks went drifting by without her giving a single thought to their original agreement. The plaster-cast came off her wrist, and with Andreas looking indulgently on, she celebrated by jumping fully clothed into the indoor swimming pool with a shriek of delight because she had been so looking forward to being able to do that. They visited London a couple of times to appear in front of an adoption panel who wanted to reassure themselves that they were, indeed, fit parents for Melanie.

But there was no problem there. For they were lovers. They were husband and wife. They were a couple in every sense of the word, which showed in the way they responded to each other.

Life was wonderful, life was great. Claire had never been so happy. And the only blot on her otherwise perfect existence was the way her aunt Laura still hadn't bothered to get in touch with her.

'I have to be in Paris for a few days from tomorrow,' Andreas informed her one morning over the breakfast table. 'Would you like to come with me?'

'Yes!' she agreed, thinking, Paris! The most romantic city in the world, and she was going to go there with the most wonderful man in the world. 'Will my aunt be there?' she questioned impulsively.

It was so many weeks since she'd watched his face close up that seeing it happen now came as a bad shock. 'We will not discuss your aunt,' he said coldly.

'But why?' Claire demanded. 'Why are you so determined to keep the two of us apart? It isn't as though she can hurt me, you know. I understand her better than you think I do.'

He got up from the table. 'We will not discuss her,' he repeated, and walked arrogantly away.

'Then I'm not coming to Paris,' she threw after him. Childish, she knew. Petty, she knew. But she felt childish and petty at that moment.

And Andreas responded accordingly—by not even faltering a single step in his retreat. She sulked for the rest of the day and he retaliated by treating her as if nothing was the matter. But when he reached for her in bed that night it was Claire who surrendered to a power much greater than her will to stand aloof from him.

The next morning she awoke to find him gone to Paris, and she felt so angry and hurt that he hadn't once attempted to change her mind about going with him that she paid him back by telephoning her aunt's London apartment. She got her answering service, which, Claire realised belatedly, she should have expected if Aunt Laura was in Paris with Andreas.

So she left a message asking her aunt to call her, then spent the next few days missing Andreas so badly that when he did arrive home she fell on him like a puppy dog who thought it had been deserted by its adored master.

A few more weeks went by. Melanie was changing fast now, becoming a real little personality with squeals and smiles, who liked to kick her legs on a blanket in the warm winter sunshine, as if her Mediterranean blood demanded it of her.

The day they received official notification that Melanie

was now their legal daughter, Claire had also begun to suspect that she might be pregnant.

That evening Andreas took her out to celebrate. Decked out in one of her elegant evening gowns and with Andreas in dinner suit and bow-tie, they spent a wonderful evening dining at a very exclusive restaurant he knew in the hills behind Rafina, where they ate food that tasted like a dream and laughed and teased and talked a lot. And as they danced close together to music composed exclusively for lovers there was a point where Claire almost confided her suspicion that she could be pregnant. Only an unwillingness to overshadow the real reason why they were out celebrating like this stopped her.

Plus the fact that she wasn't sure that she was just experiencing a small glitch in her usual smoothly running cycle.

But she was so happy. So lost in this all-encompassing love that she felt for this man of hers that by the time they drove home again that evening she was weaving delicious fantasies around the two of them that involved passionate declarations of love and a life spent making babies and growing old together. And she made love with him that night as if there were no tomorrow—sublimely unaware that, indeed, tomorrow was so very close.

The next morning, Nikos drove them into the busy sea port of Rafina. Claire had shopping to do and Andreas had several business appointments, so Nikos was to drive her back home when she was ready.

Andreas kissed her deeply before climbing out of the car and leaving her to Nikos's indulgently smiling care.

'You have made him very happy,' he replied to the questioning look he caught her giving him via the rear-view mirror. 'It is a delight to all of us who have known him for most of his life to see him like this again.'

He meant since the death of his first wife, Claire realised, and felt the tiniest suspicion of a cloud begin to shadow her little bit of clear blue sky. Then she firmly dismissed the sensation as she too clambered out of the car a few minutes later.

For this was now, not six years ago. The sun was shining. Life was great. And she wasn't going to let anything spoil it!

With the confidence of youth and a determination that it was she, Claire, who counted in his life now, she went about her shopping with her metaphorical chin high and her shining blue eyes set clear ahead—just asking to be tripped up by someone or something.

It happened sooner rather than later, too. Unexpected and unprepared for it, she walked out of the chemist shop armed with her only purchase—and stopped dead in her tracks as she came face to face with her aunt.

'Aunt Laura?' she gasped in delighted surprise.

Dressed to her usual sharp, immaculate standard, Aunt Laura looked so thoroughly disconcerted to see Claire standing there that there was a heart-stopping moment when Claire actually suspected she was going to turn away as if she didn't know her!

'Aunt Laura? It's me—Claire,' she inserted hurriedly, feeling just a little stupid for declaring herself like that.

Her aunt must have thought so too, because her expression was derisive. 'I know it's you,' she sighed. 'I'm not blind.'

But she *had* been going to turn away from her; Claire was certain about that now. And it hurt. Hurt almost as much as the realisation that if her aunt was right here in Rafina, then Andreas knew about it but hadn't bothered to tell her.

Her aunt was looking her over now, the derision more pronounced as her cool grey eyes took in the quality of Claire's casual linen jacket worn with a simple straight skirt and skinny top that still managed to shriek designer at her.

'Well, you certainly fell on your feet,' she commented tightly. 'You've caught yourself a rich man with a rich lifestyle—so who the hell can blame you for not caring if it is all just one big sham?'

'It isn't a sham,' Claire denied, stunned by the bitterness filtering through her aunt's voice. 'We're in love with each other.'

'Love?' Her aunt made a scoffing sound. 'A man like Andreas Markopoulou doesn't fall in love, Claire. He makes clear-cut, coldly calculating business decisions.'

'Stop it,' she responded, not understanding why her aunt was being so nasty. Besides Melanie, they were the only living relatives either of them had left in the world. Surely it had to count for something? But then, it never had before, had it? Claire reminded herself heavily. 'Andreas is your boss,' she said a little shakily. 'I thought you admired and respected him.'

'My—what?' Aunt Laura gasped, staring at her niece as if she'd grown an extra head. 'He isn't my boss,' she denied. 'Where the hell did you get that idea from?'

It was like standing on the edge of a precipice; Claire felt a frightening tingling sensation slither through her body right down to her toes. 'Don't play games with me.' She frowned. Why else would they bump into each other here, in Andreas's home town of all places? 'You were both on your way abroad on a business trip the first time I met him!'

'Is that what he told you?' Claire's own confused expression gave her aunt the answer to that question, and she huffed out a tightly sardonic laugh. 'You have to give it to the ruthless swine,' she allowed. 'He doesn't miss a trick. Has he told you anything, Claire?' she then asked cynically. 'Or has the smooth, slick devil managed to con you into his life and into his bed, *and* get what he really wanted from you—which was really only ever Melanie—without having to let a single family skeleton out of the family closet?'

She fell off that precipice. Standing there beneath the Greek winter-blue sky and with her feet planted firmly on solid earth, she felt herself beginning to fall a long, long way into a cold, dark place as she heard herself whisper, 'What are you talking about?'

Aunt Laura's angry gaze shifted restlessly away as if she was trying to decide whether to say any more. Then she looked back at Claire—and her face hardened. 'Why not?' she decided. 'He deserves his come-uppance, and I owe him one. So, come on...' she urged. 'Let's find somewhere less public for this, because you're in for a bad shock, and by the look of you it may be better if you receive it sitting down...'

Nikos kept sending her strange glances via his mirror as he drove her home. Claire didn't really blame him for looking at her like that. For the bright-eyed, happy person he had dropped off at the shops only an hour before had gone, and in her place was someone else entirely: a sad, pale, haunted-looking creature he had once seen before, lying in a road after she had been knocked down.

'Are you all right, *kyria*?' he enquired concernedly.

Claire's eyelashes flickered in an attempt to bring her glazed eyes into focus, but she wasn't very successful. 'Yes,' she nodded, and tried to swallow the huge lump that was blocking her throat—she wasn't very successful there either. 'A small headache, that's all. I'll be fine once I get back and take something for it.'

But she wasn't going to be fine. She knew it—and perhaps Nikos knew it, because she saw him lift his mobile phone to his ear and begin talking in Greek just before she shut herself away inside her own head again.

He was calling Andreas, she was sure. In a way she was glad. For the quicker Andreas was brought back to the house to find out what was the matter with her, the quicker she could leave it.

It wasn't far from Rafina to the house. Fifteen minutes at most. As Nikos drew the car to a stop, Claire climbed out, walked in through the front door and up the stairs without so much as glancing sideways.

In her room—*her* room, not the one she had been sharing with Andreas for the last few months or so—she came to a stop in the middle of the carpet, then coldly and precisely began stripping off the casual but chic clothes she was wearing. Leaving them to lie where they fell, she then walked naked into the dressing room hung with the kind of clothes most women only dreamed of owning. When she came back out again a few minutes later, she was wearing her old jeans and a tee shirt. In her arms she carried the rest of the clothes that she had brought with her from London and never worn since.

Now she was shutting the door on the extravagant dressing room knowing that she would never be wearing a single garment in there again.

For he could pay through the teeth for the privilege of having Melanie for his daughter, but he would never pay for the privilege of having Claire again!

She heard a car come racing up the driveway as she placed the stack of clothes on the bed, ready for packing. It was Andreas, she was sure of it, though who he had got to bring him home she had no idea—nor cared. By the time he swung in through her bedroom door, she was just placing her rings in the little velvet jewellery box where she kept all of the things his grandmother had given her.

She didn't bother to turn and look at him, but could sense him taking in at a glance the mound of discarded clothes on the floor and what she was now wearing. Only a fool would have missed the significance in the change, and Andreas was no fool.

'OK,' he said. 'Explain to me what this is about.'

'I'm leaving,' she said. Not, I'm leaving *you*, for she no longer acknowledged there was a *him* to leave. The man wasn't human. He was cast from some hard, impenetrable metal that gave him the will to do unspeakable things just to get his own way.

She heard the bedroom door close as she was rummaging in the dressing-table drawers, picking out the bits that belonged to her and leaving behind the ones that no longer did.

'Why?' he asked quietly.

She didn't answer—couldn't. It was all stopped up inside her as if someone had ground a cork into a fizzing bottle. But what really bothered her was what would happen if that same person came along and shook the damned bottle.

'Something happened in Rafina,' he prompted when she didn't say anything.

Naturally he would presume that because that was where she had been when she'd altered into a different person. Or went back to being the person she used to be, she corrected grimly.

'You saw someone...'

She could feel his footsteps vibrate through the carpet as he came towards her. Her hands began to shake badly as she pulled open another drawer.

'Desmona, perhaps. Has Desmona been stirring up trouble again, Claire?' he demanded. 'Is that what this is about?'

Try again, she thought bitterly. She picked up a framed photograph of her mother holding Melanie in her arms and made as if to edge round him.

His hand came out to touch her shoulder. 'Claire...!' he rasped out impatiently. 'This is—'

The cork blew. In a fountain spout of bitter fury, she turned on him and let fly with her hand to the side of his wretched, deceiving face. 'Don't touch me ever again—do you hear?' she spat at him.

His hand was already covering the side of his face where she'd stung him. He should have been angry—Claire would have preferred him to get angry so she could feed off it, build on what was bubbling up inside her.

But those black eyes of his just looked bewildered. And she couldn't cope with that. 'You lied to me,' she accused him thickly. 'Ever since the first day that we met you've lied and you've lied and you've lied...'

With that she managed to step around him. On trembling

legs she walked across to the bed and placed her mother's photograph on the stack of things already assembled there.

'You've seen your aunt Laura,' he realised belatedly. 'I did wonder if there was a risk of that when she turned up at my office today.'

Claire said nothing. She just stood tautly, with a white-knuckled grip on each side of the photo frame, and let the silence grow to suffocating proportions.

'What did she tell you?' he asked eventually, sounding flat and weary, like someone who knew he had been exposed without the ability to defend himself.

'She doesn't even work for you,' she whispered. 'She never did.'

'You made that assumption, Claire,' he murmured. 'All I did was allow you to go on thinking it.'

That was his defence? Claire didn't think much of it, then.

'But why?' she demanded, spinning around to lash the question at him, and so hurt by her own wretched gullibility that she couldn't keep it out of her voice. 'Why should you want to deceive me and trick me and manipulate me like this—when the truth would probably have given you the same results?'

He released a heavy sigh. His hand fell away from the side of his face and as it did so Claire felt a tiny pinch of remorse when she saw the imprint of her fingers showing white against his olive skin.

'I could not afford to take the risk that you would not fall in with my—plan,' he answered.

'Your plan to take Melanie away from me.' She spelled it out clearly.

'That was the original idea, yes.' He freely admitted it. Then his eyes flicked her a searching look. 'Your aunt told you about my brother and your mother?'

For an answer, she wrapped her arms around her slender body, her eyes closing as her mind replayed her aunt's wretched story of her mother's brief affair in Madrid with the hugely wealthy but very married fifty-year-old Greek merchant banker, Timo Markopoulou, which had resulted in Melanie.

'I'm sorry,' she heard him mutter.

What for? she wondered. For being responsible for making her feel like this, or was he apologising on behalf of his brother and her mother?

'Did you know about their affair while it was happening?' she whispered threadily.

'I knew about an affair—yes,' he confirmed, turning away from her to go and stare grimly out of the window. 'But I did not know who the woman involved was,' he went on. 'Or the fact that she had borne him a child, until almost a year after Timo's death and I was in London on business when your aunt came to see me.'

Claire's eyes flicked open, the blue bright with a derision she speared at his profile. 'You mean you went to see my aunt,' she corrected him. 'To get her to bargain with me for possession of Melanie!'

'Is that what she said?' His dark head turned. 'Then she lied,' he declared, holding her sceptical gaze with a grim demand that she believe him. 'Your aunt Laura approached me, Claire,' he insisted. 'It was she who told me that my brother's mistress had given birth to his daughter. It was she who wanted to bargain—not for Melanie,' he made succinctly clear, 'but for your silence about the affair. *Your* silence, Claire,' he sombrely repeated. 'Your aunt placed herself in the role of mere mediator between myself and her *niece*—the niece she swore had been my dead brother's mistress!'

'M-me?' she stammered in shocked confusion. 'My aunt told you that *I* was your brother's mistress?'

Her sense of horror and dismay was obvious. Andreas acknowledged her right to feel like that with a tight-lipped grimace. 'Apparently you were threatening to sell the story to the papers if I did not pay for your silence,' he explained.

'But how could you think such terrible things about me?' Claire cried.

'I had not met you then,' he reminded her. 'So I gained an impression of a grasping young woman who saw her child's wealthy Greek relatives as a pushover for a bit of lucrative blackmail.'

It made a kind of sense. Claire felt sick suddenly. Sick with shame at her aunt's mercenary cunning.

'I could not afford to risk such a scandal breaking in the press when my grandmother was so frail,' he continued, whilst, white as a sheet now, Claire stared blindly at the floor. 'The one thing your aunt could not have known was my grandmother's dream to hold her great-grandchild before she died. But it was only a dream,' he sighed, turning back to the window. 'Both she and I knew she didn't have a chance of fulfilling it...'

He meant because his grandmother's days had already been numbered, Claire realised sadly. 'Learning about Melanie must have seemed like a heaven-sent opportunity, then.'

The dark head nodded. 'I offered to take the child off your hands for a—certain amount of money,' he told her. 'Your aunt led me to believe that you would not be averse to the idea of giving up the burden of caring for Melanie—for the right price.'

Nice of her, Claire thought bitterly. The whole thing was a macabre circle of deceit, betrayal and greed, she acknowledged with a terrible shudder.

'So you drove her over to my flat then sat outside it in your big limousine, and waited for her to buy your brother's child for you,' she concluded, beginning to feel more than a little sick now as the rest fell into place without needing to be dragged out and pawed over.

She'd come running out of her flat and got herself knocked over in front of him. He had then been given the opportunity to see where she lived and how she lived, and eventually learned that not only was she innocent of any charge of extortion, but that he would have a hell of a job convincing her to give her sister up to him!

So then came the next round of lies, she continued while he remained silently staring out of the window, perhaps doing the same as she, and replaying the whole thing scene by miserable scene! The proposition, the coercion, the sob story gauged to tug at her tender heartstrings about a grandmother who wanted to hold her only great-grandchild before she passed away.

The only bit of truth in among all the lies, she noted cynically.

'Did your grandmother know whose child Melanie is?' she asked huskily.

He didn't answer for a moment, and there was something very—odd about his hesitation. It smacked at another lie on the way, Claire judged, eyeing him suspiciously.

'She—guessed,' he said in the end.

Truth or lie? Claire wondered. 'You devil,' his grandmother had said to him, she recalled, and got to her feet as an icy chill went washing through her.

What a waste of all his efforts, she mused acidly. For by then the wedding had taken place, otherwise he could have saved himself a whole lot of inconvenience. Then she remembered that Andreas had still needed to acquire legal control of his brother's illegitimate child. So—not such a waste of his time.

'Did you pay my aunt to keep away from me?' she asked.

'Yes,' he admitted. 'The reason why she started this was because she had lost her job, was in a terrible amount of debt, and she saw me as a quick way to get herself out of trouble. But she then proceeded to lose the money trying to double it by speculating on the markets.'

'So she came to your office today wanting more.'

'I kicked her out,' he stated flatly. 'She took her revenge.

I should have expected it—being a ruthless rat myself dealing with one of my kind.'

Which seemed to round it all off pretty well, Claire thought as the pain in her breast eased to a dull ache.

'I never did any of this to hurt you, Claire,' he murmured, as if he could sense what she was feeling. 'Though you probably find it impossible to believe right now, I acted with your interests at heart also.'

It was impossible, she agreed. People who had your interests at heart did not lie, cheat and plot to steal from you.

'Your aunt intended to give me Melanie, take the money and run,' he told her. 'I could not have done that to you,' he added huskily. 'I only had to know you for half an hour to realise I could not have done it. So I lied,' he admitted. 'I gave you what you seemed to need then, which was a reason worthy of you staying within my protection. Think about it,' he urged. 'When has anything I've done—lies or truth—actually been done to deliberately hurt you?'

Silence met that. The kind of silence that throbbed and pulled and prodded at the self-control she was having to exert over herself not to break down and cry all over him.

'Stay,' he fed gently into that silence. 'Don't let yourself be manoeuvred by a cold and embittered woman who has never done anything but hurt you...'

'I can't think straight,' she whispered, pushing a hand up to her aching eyes. 'I need time to come to terms with all of this before I make a decision as to whether I stay or go.'

Andreas seemed to draw himself up. 'Fair enough,' he agreed, and his tone altered, cooled, and became businesslike. 'Take your time,' he invited. 'There is no rush.'

With that he began to walk away. Making the tactical retreat, Claire recognised as she watched him with the tears already splitting her vision into a million fragmented parts.

Halfway to the door the toe of his shoe caught something that lay on the floor amongst the debris of her recently discarded clothes. Through the blur of tears she watched him pause and glance down, watched him go still for a moment before be bent to pick something up. It never occurred to her what that something was—until she heard the tearing of flimsy paper.

And, on a lightning shot of panic, she was galvanised into action, darting across the room in an effort to snatch the pregnancy testing kit out of his hands before he realised what it was he was looking at!

Too late. He spun to stare at her. Her heart sank to the soles of her feet. He'd gone white—perfectly, sickeningly white. 'Why have you bought this?' he demanded hoarsely.

He might be white, but Claire wasn't; she was blushing like a schoolgirl. 'Please give it to me,' she insisted, holding out a badly trembling hand.

'*Why?*' he barked.

The sheer ferocity of it thoroughly shocked her. Her blue eyes widened in surprise, and she began backing away, cautiously—bewilderedly. Not understanding the need for this depth of anger.

'Answer me,' he commanded forcefully. 'Answer me, Claire!'

'I w-would have told you,' she stammered shakily. 'If—if it w-was positive.' Was that why he was so angry—because he believed she'd intended to hide it from him? 'I would have told you, Andreas!' she repeated shrilly when he actually took a step towards her.

'I want you out of this house,' he hissed furiously at her. 'Within the hour, do you hear me? I want you gone from my sight and I never want to see you again!'

'But—why are you so angry?' Claire shrilled, still backing while he paced towards her like a wild animal needing to taste fresh blood. 'We haven't used protection once in all the weeks we've been making love! Surely you must have considered this a strong possibility?'

'And I used to get these damned things shoved in my face once a month by my first wife!' he rasped. 'For five hellish years, I used to listen to her sob her heart out once a month when the damn things told her what we both already knew! I am infertile, Claire!' he raked rawly at her—watched her face blanch in shock, and tossed the packet aside in disgust.

The dreadful words held her still and shaking, confusion and horror warring for dominance on her face. 'I know you said you never wanted children of your own,' she whispered. 'But...I *feel* pregnant, Andreas!' she cried out pleadingly.

'So did Sofia,' he growled. 'Every single wretched month.'

'No...' she breathed, refusing to take on board what he was saying here. 'I'm not like her—I'm not!' she insisted as those hard black eyes flicked her a contemptuous look. 'I love you!' she cried, saying the words out loud for the very first time in her desperation. 'I couldn't hurt you by playing on your feelings like that!'

'Sofia loved me,' he replied. 'She worshipped the ground that I walked upon! She leaned on me—lived for me!' A harshly grating sound of scornful laughter escaped him. 'And in the end she even decided to put me out of my misery by killing herself in the name of *love!*'

That was six years ago, and he still has not recovered from what that final act of rank selfishness did to his soul, she realised.

She was so white in the face now that she began to look like marble. 'I don't want to believe all of this...' she breathed as if in a crazed nightmare.

'Then make yourself believe,' he advised her coldly. 'For I am infertile and this marriage is over. I will not be put through that kind of hell again—not for you—not for any woman,' he concluded as he strode angrily for the door.

This time he passed through it without any hesitation. The door closed behind him, leaving Claire standing there, trembling from the top of her head to the soles of her feet as she tried desperately to come to terms with all the ugliness and horror that had been unveiled in this room today.

Infertile...

With her head turning on a neck that was too locked by stress to make the movement a smooth one, she stared dazedly at the flat packet now lying on the bed where he had tossed it. What to her had been a silly purchase made in the excitement of the moment was an instrument of torture to Andreas.

She shuddered, hating the very sight of it now, and was about to turn away from it in sickened distaste, when something he had said suddenly stilled her.

Make yourself believe, Andreas had said.

Make yourself believe...

Feeling her heart turn to stone in appalled dismay at what she was daring to consider, Claire picked up the packet.

The fierce roar of a car racing away from the house filled her head as she walked grimly into her bathroom.

CHAPTER ELEVEN

It was very late by the time his car swung back into the driveway. Huddled inside a warm winter coat, Claire was sitting on one of the pale blue upholstered chairs on the front terrace, where she had been waiting for him for what seemed like hours now.

He had to have seen her sitting there because his car headlights had picked her out as he'd driven by on his way to the garages. Yet long, long minutes went by before his tall, dark figure loomed up at her from the inky darkness.

And her first response when she looked up at him was a cold little shiver. 'Still here, I see,' he drawled.

'I needed to ask you a question before I left,' she explained. 'So I decided to wait until you got back.'

'You mean there is a lie we forgot to rake over?' he mocked.

'Maybe.' She smiled a little sadly. 'I'm not sure... Will you at least sit down and listen?' she then requested. 'Only it's very difficult to talk to someone who is bent on cutting you to ribbons with their eyes while you speak.'

He smiled that smile she hated so much, and for a moment she thought he was going to tell her to go to hell. The tension soared, filling the cool winter night with a hostility that clutched at her throat.

Maybe it did something similar to him, because he released a taut sigh as if attempting to dispel the feeling, then in the next moment was reluctantly dropping down into the chair next to her.

'Fire away,' he grimly invited.

But now that she had his attention she found she'd lost the courage to say what she wanted to say. Ironic, really, she

173

mused, when you think how many hours I've waited so patiently for this moment.

'Nice evening?' she asked, merely as a cover while she got her courage back.

His dark head turned to look at her delicately drawn profile. She looked so pale, her skin seemed to glow ghost-like in the darkness. 'Is that the question?' he enquired. 'Or just an extra one you decided to throw in?'

In other words, he was not going to make this easier for her, Claire noted. 'I am not naturally a cruel or vindictive person, Andreas,' she murmured soberly. 'I did not set out to deliberately hurt you today.'

'Now that definitely was not a question,' he clipped.

And he *definitely* was not going to make this easy. At which point she decided to just hit him with it and wait to see what he did.

'Have you been making love to me for all of these weeks just for the hell of it because I was there and so obviously willing?' she asked. 'Or did you actually let yourself care something for me *before* you allowed things to go that far?'

He shifted restlessly, so his chair creaked on the tiled terrace floor. From the way his jaw clenched, he didn't like the question and liked even less having to offer an answer.

'I did not make love to you for the hell of it,' he said.

Claire sat there beside him and smothered the urge to sigh loudly in relief as she felt a huge weight lift from her shoulders because, if he had not done it for the hell of it, then he must care—even if he never actually said that he did.

'Then may I stay?' she requested huskily. 'Please?'

He made a jerky movement with his head that made her feel as if she'd hit him again. 'You said one question,' he gritted. 'That makes two.'

So she rephrased it. 'I'll go if you want me to, but I prefer to stay. I *need* to stay here with you.'

'And Melanie, of course,' he cynically mocked.

Claire's blue eyes flashed, glinting a warning at his hard

profile. 'Don't bring Melanie into this,' she admonished. 'What is best for Melanie is a separate issue. I am talking about *me* here. *My* needs.' She tersely pressed the point. 'What *I* am going to do!'

'And you want to stay,' he drawled with crushing derision. 'How very—saintly of you, considering who you would be staying with.'

'Do you think that by mocking both me and yourself in the same sentence you will force me to hate you enough to leave *without* you having to tell me to go?' she demanded.

'I thought I had already done that,' he remarked, saw her wince, and with a sigh relented in his acid tone a little. 'Listen to me, Claire,' he prompted heavily. 'You are generous and loving and selflessly kind,' he told her. 'But you are also young and extremely beautiful. If you leave here now, you will soon pick up the threads of your own life, eventually meet a lucky man one day who will fulfil your heart's desire in every single way. But I am not that man,' he stated gruffly. 'I am too old for you, too—flawed, and just too cynical for someone as fresh and perfect as you.'

'But you aren't saying that you wouldn't like to be that lucky man,' she said. 'Only that you don't think you can be him.'

His laugh was soft and rueful. 'I forgot to say stubborn, too,' he murmured—only to tag on harshly, 'Why can't you make this easier on both of us and accept that I am not going to let you stay with me?'

'Because I love you,' she replied. 'Though I don't think you deserve it. Or you couldn't be trying to hurt me like this. And if you dare to quote the cruel to be kind thing at me,' she added warningly, 'I will probably hit you again—old man.'

'Then I won't say it,' he promised. 'But neither will I change my mind.'

He sounded so strong, so—resolved, her heart gave a painful little lurch in response to it. 'So, if I get up right now and walk off into that darkness leaving Melanie behind—which is what you only ever really wanted—will that make you happy, Andreas? Will it?'

He didn't answer, but she could feel the sharp increase in his tension. On impulse she stood up—could have wept when his hand snaked out to capture hers and he muttered, 'No,' so rawly that it rasped over his throat like sandpaper, and his grip was intense.

In a flurry of shaking limbs she spun around to come and squat down in front of him. Her hair had grown longer over the last couple of months, grown thicker and glossier so that even here, in the darkness of the terrace, it shone like golden syrup around the tense pallor of her face as she tried to capture his eyes. Only he wouldn't let her do that—hadn't, in fact, since he'd appeared in front of her tonight. And that made her hurt for him, because she understood why he would not meet her gaze.

It was wretched—utterly wretched.

'OK,' she murmured shakily. 'New scenario—right?' Her free hand went up, ice-cold and trembling fingertips touching the white ring of tension circling his mouth. 'You meet a girl, you fall in love with her. You ask her to marry you. She turns round and tells you that she can't have children. Do you just walk away, Andreas?' she asked him gently. 'Does the fact that she can't give you children suddenly make her less worthy of your love?'

'This is a senseless exercise,' he gritted, dislodging her fingers with a tense movement of his head. 'Simply because it is not the case here.'

'How do you know?' Claire challenged. 'How can either you or I know whether I don't have my own flaw that will stop me from conceiving? When it has never been put to the test?'

'And never will be by me,' he uttered grimly.

'But that isn't the point I was trying to make,' she pressed. 'Are you saying that when this fantastic new man comes along to sweep me off my feet I have to have him checked out to see if he's fertile before I fall in love with him? And that he has to do the same with me?'

'Don't be foolish.' He began to scowl. 'And stop this line of argument right now. For I refuse to play mind games with ifs, buts and maybes. Why can't you simply accept that I am not going to let you stay here with me?'

'Then why are you holding so tightly to my hand?' Claire countered softly.

His hand snapped away from her, his hard face darkening with a sudden loss of patience. 'I've had enough of this,' he muttered, going to get up.

But Claire beat him to it. 'So have I,' she agreed, straightening away from him before he could stand up. 'So I am going to go to my lonely bed to dream of wildly exciting men with very high sperm counts,' she bitterly informed him. 'And you never know—if I dream hard enough, by the time morning comes around, I may have managed to purge my love for you right out of me! Then leaving here tomorrow could well turn out to be a pleasure!'

With that she stalked into the house, leaving him sitting there alone with only his stubborn pride to help him mull over what she had just said.

On reaching her room, she stripped off her clothes and climbed into bed, closed her eyes and, with gritted teeth, waited to see if her angry words managed to shock a reaction out of him.

Sure enough, a couple of minutes later, the door to his own room slammed shut, and a few more minutes after that the connecting door flew open. Claire refused to open her eyes.

'You asked for this,' he growled, coming to lean over her. 'You wanted to make me angry—well, I'm angry,' he confirmed as his naked body slid between the sheets. 'You wanted to make me jealous,' he added as he reached out for her. 'Well, I am damned well jealous!'

'Of my dreams?' she taunted, opening her eyes.

'Of everything to do with you!' he rasped, and imprisoned her very willing mouth.

It became a battle of wills as to who could arouse the other more. He kissed and licked and teased her, and shrouded her in the heaviest kind of sensuality. And she returned everything with interest, driving him out of control with the touch of her mouth and the caress of her fingers and the soft urgency with which she whispered her desire to him. 'Will my other men make me feel as good as this?' she dared to question curiously.

Her innocence before he came along added immense power to the question. But it was dangerous, it was reckless. He responded by entering her like a man who had lost touch with his sanity.

And as he drove her before him into the same wild place she thought she heard an anguished whimper, and realised with a sense of wretched guilt that the sound had come from him.

'I don't leave tomorrow, then?' she murmured when it was all over and she was lying curled close up against him, his arms still wrapped around her as if they couldn't let go.

'You stay until you are ready to go,' he replied. 'I refuse to accept more than that from you.'

Very magnanimous, Claire thought, and broke herself free from his arms to walk off to her own bathroom. When she came back she had something hidden in the palm of her hand—though he didn't notice that because he was too busy absorbing every nuance of her slender shape as she came back to him.

Straddling his lean waist, she sat looking thoughtfully down at his dark face. His eyes were hooded again—but lazily, their dark depths gleaming with a deliciously greedy possessiveness as they looked at her body.

'I have something to tell you,' she confessed. 'But I need you to promise me that you won't get angry.'

'Strange request, that,' he drawled, lifting up his arms to fold them beneath his head. 'I feel myself growing angry at the mere suggestion.'

'I thought you might.' She grimaced, sighed and then began. 'I've had a very bad day today,' she informed him. 'Almost the worst of my life.'

'My fault, I presume.'

'Hmm... Yes and no,' she replied. 'Meeting my aunt didn't help. Then you and I rowed and you took off like a maniac. I was feeling pretty miserable by then, I can tell you.'

'I'm sorry,' he sighed.

She shrugged the apology away. 'Then something really frightening happened,' she told him. 'So I got Nikos to take me back to Rafina so I could visit a doctor.'

His eyes sharpened, his arms dropped down so his hands could clasp her around her waist. 'Why?' he raked at her. 'What happened to you?'

'He examined me,' she explained as if he hadn't spoken. 'Confirmed my worst fears... You do trust me, don't you, Andreas, not to have ever been unfaithful to you?' she then asked carefully.

'Of course.' He frowned, impatient with what he saw as an irrelevance, coming as it did right in the middle of what she was telling him. 'Stop making a meal of this,' he rasped. 'And tell me what the hell is wrong with you!'

'M-my uterus is enlarged,' she said, not finding this as easy as she'd expected it to be. 'H-he did some tests.' She took a deep breath, then let it out again. 'I'm—I'm pregnant,' she announced.

It took a moment, while Claire sat there across him and waited with bated breath. Then he uttered a very rude word, and in an act of blind fury he toppled her off his chest and launched himself out of the bed. 'I thought you had agreed not to do this!' he bit out as he paced angrily away from her.

'S-six weeks to be exact,' Claire continued unsteadily. 'Andreas—I need you to—'

'How many times do I have to go through this hell?' he raged right over the top of whatever she'd been going to say. 'You cannot be pregnant!' he turned to blast at her. 'I am infertile, for goodness' sake! I am *infertile*!'

Trembling too much to dare try to stand up and go to him, Claire drew up her knees and hugged them to her chest. 'The doctor explained that,' she murmured shakily.

He went off in a fury of Greek.

Sitting there like that, Claire closed her eyes tightly and waited for the furious stream to stop before grimly forcing herself to continue. 'He said that research into male infertility is relatively new. That they are only just discovering that a man's sperm count can change virtually by the m-month.'

'I'm not listening to this.' Reeling almost drunkenly, he made for his own room.

'H-he said if you only did the test once,' she stammered after him, 'then you could have just chosen an unlucky day!'

'An unlucky day?' he repeated, coming to a taut standstill. Then he twisted his dark head to look at her. What she saw written on his face made her insides shrivel. 'I had five years of unlucky days, Claire,' he reminded her bitterly. 'Try talking your way around that.'

She nodded, and swallowed, her blue eyes determined even while they swam with tears. 'Ap-apparently he used to be Sofia's family doctor,' she explained. 'He...'

'No.' Andreas immediately denied that. 'Our family doctor is in Athens—'

'And *this* doctor was Sofia's family practitioner *before* she married you!' Claire inserted. 'He—he w-wants to talk to you—confidentially,' she told him. 'H-he says he has some information y-you may like to hear ab-about Sofia...'

Something happened, Claire wasn't sure exactly what, but something most certainly cracked that death mask he was wearing clamped over his face—before he turned and walked into his own room without a word.

She wilted like a dying swan, her long neck folding over her knees. Her heart was pounding heavily, her lungs almost completely locked inside the tension surrounding them. And her brain seemed to have closed itself down altogether, because she could not think of a single thing beyond that expression on his wretched face as he'd walked away.

Something landed on the bed beside her. Her head shot up, blue eyes despairingly vulnerable as they searched out his. But Andreas had shut off completely. 'Ring him,' he commanded.

'Ring who?' She frowned in confusion.

'This—doctor.' A long, taut finger pointed stabbingly at something beside her on the bed; glancing dazedly down, Claire saw it was a mobile telephone.

'But it's the middle of the night,' she protested.

'Then wake him up,' he insisted.

When she still didn't make a move to do his bidding, he bent to snatch the telephone back again. 'What's the bloody number?' he grated.

'I d-don't know,' she confessed. 'All I did was ask Nikos to take me to see a doctor and he drove me there...'

'His name, then,' he flicked tightly at her. 'You do at least know the name of this doctor you allowed to make an intimate examination of you?'

'An appointment card,' she suddenly remembered. 'Over there on the dressing table.'

Grimly he went to find it with hard fingers scattering things anywhere they fell. In that kind of tight, staccato way, he read the Greek symbols printed on the card, and stabbed them into his mobile.

Claire couldn't sit there and take any more. She climbed off the bed and escaped into her bathroom, where she sat on the toilet seat and shivered while she listened to his deep voice firing questions at the poor doctor in Greek.

Then the silence came back. She continued to sit there, not sure what to do, until her flesh grew so cold she had to get up and pull on her bathrobe. Shoving her hands into the cavernous pockets, she allowed herself a couple of deep breaths for courage, then let herself into the bedroom again.

Andreas was sitting on the end of her bed, slumped over with his face buried in his hands. In all her life she had never seen anything so wretched as this proud Greek man reduced to this.

Without a second thought, she went over there, climbed onto the bed behind him then simply wrapped her arms around him as tightly as she could.

'She lied to me,' he murmured hoarsely.

'I know,' Claire softly replied.

'She knew even before she married me that she was not able to conceive, yet she put me through all of that—torment. Month after month.' He laboured the point, dragging his hands away from his face so he could use them to help him. 'She made me feel useless and helpless and...'

It all came pouring out then. While Claire knelt behind him and held onto him tightly, Andreas drew a vivid picture of what it had been like to live with a woman whose obsessive need to bear a child had turned both their lives into a living nightmare. Not once had Sofia suggested the fault could be hers. Loving him and living in fear of losing him, she had created a web of deceit that involved cruel tricks and lies which kept him balanced on a knife-edge of failure and despair. By the time he had been driven into taking a fertility test himself, the sheer stress of it all must have lowered his count.

'She took a terrible risk, allowing you to take that test,' Claire pointed out soberly.

'Not really,' Andreas contended. 'Either way, the torment would have continued. With a strong count she would have merely increased her efforts to conceive. A low count gave her a similar excuse to—be lucky one day—as she loved to say to me.' A shudder ripped through him; Claire tightened her hold on him. 'In the end I couldn't bring myself to touch her, I felt such a pitiful failure,' he admitted. 'I think my withdrawal from her bed was what finally tipped her over the edge.'

And left him with yet another sense of failure he had to learn to live with, Claire realised sadly.

'I'm so sorry,' she murmured.

His shoulders flexed. 'What have you got to be sorry for?' he demanded. 'It should be me apologising to you for the way I behaved before!'

'I understood.'

'You're pregnant...' he husked suddenly.

'Mmm,' she softly confirmed. 'Are you pleased?'

He rubbed his hands over his face. 'Shell-shocked, I think,' he admitted, but some of the tension began to ease out of him.

'I have something for you,' she said, and, taking the pen-shaped tester out of her pocket, she gravely handed it to him over his shoulder. 'Our baby,' she confided. 'What do you think—boy or girl?'

She tried to keep it light, but she could feel the emotion come roaring up inside him as he sat there staring down at that silly little indicator that had been such a source of pain to him before now.

When he moved, he did it with a throaty growl as he twisted around and tumbled her onto the bed. 'From the moment you opened your lovely blue eyes on a dusty road back in London, I knew you were going to mean something special to me,' he told her deeply. 'But I never dared to so much as dream of anything *this* special.'

'Here,' Claire invited. 'Feel for yourself just how special...' And, taking hold of his hand, she fed it between their bodies so she could press his palm against her womb. There was nothing to show for the miracle taking place inside her, of course—it was much too soon—but the gesture itself was

enough to have her drowning in the intense darkness of his
wonderful eyes.

'I am going to love you until the day I die,' he vowed.
'And I am never going to let you go.'

'I've been trying very hard not to get away, please note,'
she pointed out gently.

'Stubborn,' he accused her softly.

'In love,' she amended.

For that, he kissed her. Kissed her long and deep and with
a heart-stirring tenderness that told her more than anything
else could do just how much he loved to hear her say that.

Timo Markopoulou arrived in the world very early on a
bright and hot summer morning.

His mother was exhausted, but she couldn't allow herself
to fall asleep. She was too busy observing the way Andreas
was sitting in the chair by her bed, with Melanie seated on
one half of his lap while his small son occupied the other.

He was introducing them to each other, his voice softly
reassuring though both babies were too young to understand.
Yet, sitting there on his lap, gazing solemnly at her new
brother who looked remarkably like herself when she was
born, Melanie seemed to understand something of what her
papa was saying, because she reached out with a small hand
and touched the baby's cheek in just the same way Claire
had always done to her.

The incredibly gentle act from one so young had a lump
forming in Claire's throat. It affected Andreas too; she saw
the waves of love and pride go washing through him as he
caught the little girl's hand and carried it to his lips.

Lifting his head, he caught her watching them, and Claire
sent him a soft, understanding smile, but he didn't smile
back. There was just too much emotion at work inside him
for him to smile right now.

'My cup runneth over,' he murmured deeply.

That was all; his feelings at that moment required no further explanation. Needing to make a physical link with those feelings, Claire reached out to rest a hand on one of his wide shoulders. He acknowledged it by brushing it with his cheek as his attention returned to his children.

And that was the image Claire took with her as she drifted into slumber. Her love. Her life, encapsulated in that one special moment. Her own cup of happiness was overflowing too.

If you enjoyed what you just read,
then we've got an offer you can't resist!

Take 2 bestselling
love stories FREE!
Plus get a FREE surprise gift!

Coming Next Month

THE BEST HAS JUST GOTTEN BETTER!

#2109 THE MILLIONAIRE'S VIRGIN Anne Mather
Nikolas has obviously not forgiven Paige for walking out on him
four years ago. So why has he offered her a job on his Greek island
for the summer? And what exactly will he be expecting from her?

#2110 THE CATTLE KING'S MISTRESS Emma Darcy
Nathan King, powerful head of his family's cattle empire, wants
Miranda, but doubts she'll cope with outback life. Miranda wants
Nathan, too, but believes her past will deny her the chance of a
future with a King. Yet the passion between them is
overwhelming....

#2111 LUC'S REVENGE Catherine George
Devastatingly attractive Luc Brissac was not only interested in
buying Portia's childhood home—scene of something so traumatic
she had blotted it from her memory—he was determined to have
Portia, as well! But when Luc took her back to France as his future
bride, the past went with them....

#2112 THE MISTRESS DECEPTION Susan Napier
When Rachel had innocently offered to undress Matthew Riordan
after a party, she didn't expect to find herself being blackmailed!
Matthew certainly wanted her as his mistress—but was he driven
by desire or deception?

#2113 A SUSPICIOUS PROPOSAL Helen Brooks
Millionaire businessman Xavier Grey seemed intent on pursuing
Essie. And he was used to getting what he wanted! But when he
proposed, was it an affair or marriage he had in mind...and could
Essie trust him?

#2114 AN INNOCENT AFFAIR Kim Lawrence
Everything had looked set for Hope's marriage to gorgeous tycoon
Alex Matheson—until the rumors started. As a top international
model, Hope was used to tabloid speculation. But now she *had* to
convince Alex of her innocence....

CNM0500